A TIDE WORTH TURNING

A SURF'S UP ROMANCE NOVELLA

BETH WISEMAN

A TIDE WORTH TURNING

Cover design: Elizabeth Wiseman Mackey

Interior design: Elizabeth Wiseman Mackey

To Jamie Foley

ACCLAIM FOR BETH WISEMAN

Home All Along

"Beth Wiseman's novel will find a permanent home in every reader's heart as she spins comfort and prose into a stellar read of grace."

—*Kelly Long, author of the Patch of Heaven series*

Love Bears All Things

"Suggest to those seeking a more truthful, less saccharine portrayal of the trials of human life and the transformative growth and redemption that may occur as a result."

—*Library Journal*

Her Brother's Keeper

"Wiseman has created a series in which the readers have a chance to peel back all the layers of the Amish secrets."

—*RT Book Reviews, 4 1/2 stars and July 2015 Top Pick!*

"Wiseman's new launch is edgier, taking on the tough issues of mental illness and suicide. Amish fiction fans seeking something a bit more thought-provoking and challenging than the usual fare will find this series debut a solid choice."

—*Library Journal*

The Promise

"The story of Mallory in The Promise uncovers the harsh reality American women can experience when they follow their hearts into a very different culture. Her story sheds light on how Islamic society is totally different from the Christian marriage covenant between one man and one woman. This novel is based on actual events, and Beth reached out to me during that time. It was heartbreaking to watch those real-life events unfolding. I salute the author's courage, persistence, and final triumph in writing a revealing and inspiring story."

—*Nonie Darwish, author of The Devil We Don't Know, Cruel and Usual Punishment, and Now They Call Me Infidel*

"The Promise is an only too realistic depiction of an American young woman motivated by the best humanitarian impulses and naïve trust facing instead betrayal, kidnapping, and life-threatening danger in Pakistan's lawless Pashtun tribal regions. But the story offers as well a reminder just as realistic that love and sacrifice are never wasted and that the hope of a loving heavenly Father is never absent in the most hopeless of situations."

—*Jeanette Windle, author of Veiled Freedom (2010 ECPA Christian Book Award/Christy Award finalist), Freedom's*

Stand (2012 *ECPA Christian Book Award/Carol Award finalist*), *and Congo Dawn* (2013 *Golden Scroll Novel of the Year*)

The House that Love Built

"This sweet story with a hint of mystery is touching and emotional. Humor sprinkled throughout balances the occasional seriousness. The development of the love story is paced perfectly so that the reader gets a real sense of the characters."

—*RT Book Reviews, 4 stars*

"[The House that Love Built] is a warm, sweet tale of faith renewed and families restored."

—*BookPage*

Need You Now

"Wiseman, best known for her series of Amish novels, branches out into a wider world in this story of family, dependence, faith, and small-town Texas, offering a character for every reader to relate to . . . With an enjoyable cast of outside characters, Need You Now breaks the molds of small-town stereotypes. With issues ranging from special education and teen cutting to what makes a marriage strong, this is a compelling and worthy read."

—*Booklist*

"Wiseman gets to the heart of marriage and family interests in a way that will resonate with readers, with an intricately written plot featuring elements that seem to be ripped from current headlines. God provides hope for Wiseman's characters even in the most desperate situations."

—*RT Book Reviews, 4 stars*

"You may think you are familiar with Beth's wonderful story-telling gift but this is something new! This is a story that will stay with you for a long, long time. It's a story of hope when life seems hopeless. It's a story of how God can redeem the seemingly unredeemable. It's a message the Church, the world needs to hear."

—*Sheila Walsh, author of God Loves Broken People*

"Beth Wiseman tackles these difficult subjects with courage and grace. She reminds us that true healing can only come by being vulnerable and honest before our God who loves us more than anything."

—*Deborah Bedford, bestselling author of His Other Wife, A Rose by the Door, and The Penny (coauthored with Joyce Meyer)*

The Land of Canaan Novels

"Wiseman's voice is consistently compassionate and her words flow smoothly."

—*Publishers Weekly review of Seek Me with All Your Heart*

"Wiseman's third Land of Canaan novel overflows with romance, broken promises, a modern knight in shining armor, and hope at the end of the rainbow."

—*RT Book Reviews*

"In Seek Me with All Your Heart, Beth Wiseman offers readers a heartwarming story filled with complex characters and deep emotion. I instantly loved Emily, and eagerly turned each page, anxious to learn more about her past—and what future the Lord had in store for her."

—*Shelley Shepard Gray, bestselling author of the Seasons of Sugarcreek series*

"Wiseman has done it again! Beautifully compelling, Seek Me with All Your Heart is a heartwarming story of faith, family, and renewal. Her characters and descriptions are captivating, bringing the story to life with the turn of every page."

—*Amy Clipston, bestselling author of A Gift of Grace*

The Daughters of the Promise Novels

"Well-defined characters and story make for an enjoyable read."

—*RT Book Reviews on Plain Pursuit*

"A touching, heartwarming story. Wiseman does a particularly great job of dealing with shunning, a controversial Amish practice that seems cruel and unnecessary to outsiders . . . If you're a fan of Amish fiction, don't miss Plain Pursuit!"

—*Kathleen Fuller, author of The Middlefield Family novels*

CHAPTER 1

Addison paced across her mother's living room as sweat dampened her temples and the base of her neck. May was already punishing them with Texas temperatures that were usually reserved for July and August. But Lee Ann Burke had a steadfast rule not to run the air conditioning until July. If there was any saving grace at all, it was the ocean pushing a breeze ashore, which wafted through the screened windows of the house Addison had grown up in. She breathed in the briny aroma, a smell she'd haul to her grave someday, with enough good and bad memories to keep her balanced on the plank she'd been walking since her father died.

She glanced at her smartphone, wondering if she was going to make it to her next appointment on time. The continuous drip of the kitchen faucet around the corner felt like water torture against her left temple. She rubbed the source of the irritation. "Mom, are you sure the agency said three o'clock? It's almost three thirty."

"That's what they said." Her mother didn't glance up, but

kept focused on the jigsaw puzzle she was hunched over. Addison couldn't recall a time that her family—small as it was—had ever shared a meal at the kitchen table, except maybe Christmas and Thanksgiving. On most days, her mother had one of her puzzles spread atop the oak table, with a sweating glass of sweet tea nearby and an ashtray. There was still sweat tea within reach, but at least Mom had taken to smoking her cigarettes outside a few years ago, something she should have done when it became common knowledge that secondhand smoke was unhealthy. Addison recalled all the smoke she and her father had inhaled over the years, wondering if that might have contributed to her father's cancer diagnosis. Addison could still smell the stench of tobacco in the house. In light of recent events, she wondered if her mother would quit smoking. *Doubtful.* If she didn't quit after they found out Dad had cancer, Addison doubted she'd do it now.

Addison glanced at the TV trays in the stand next to the couch, the rust barely visible amidst the flowery design that vined up the legs and covered the tops. She couldn't help but smile. Some of her happiest moments were in this living room eating on TV trays and watching "Everyone Loves Raymond." Her father had loved that show, and sometimes Addison could almost hear her father's laughter late at night, right before she drifted off to sleep. Maybe he was sending her a message that she'd laugh again one day too.

Sighing, she walked to the window to get the full effect of the breeze, and after another twenty minutes of pacing the living room, she was glad to see a car turning in the driveway. "Mom, the caregiver from the agency is here." She turned to face her mother, who still didn't look up. "Mom, did you hear me?"

Slowly, her mother pulled her eyes up until they were locked with Addison's. "I had a stroke, Addie, I'm not deaf." Scowling, she looked back at her puzzle, then mumbled, "And I don't need a babysitter."

Addison shook her head, feeling a trickle of perspiration roll down her face. They'd had this conversation a dozen times, at least. "I know you don't need a babysitter, and this woman isn't being hired for that. She's just here for a few weeks, to make sure you don't fall again and to help around the house. Just until you get your strength back."

When her mother didn't respond, Addison wound around the coffee table and moved toward the front door, surprised to see a man standing on the other side of the screen. "Can I help you?"

"G'day. I'm Logan Northrupp. The agency sent me to . . ." He unfolded a piece of paper, scanned it, then looked at Addison. "This is 222 Beachfront Drive, right? I'm here to take care of Lee Ann Burke."

It took Addison a few seconds to realize he'd said "good day." It sounded like "goodie." Addison didn't say anything for a few moments, even though she heard a slight chuckle from her mother. "Uh . . . I guess I just assumed they were sending a woman."

Mom cleared her throat. "To assume is to make an—"

"Mother!" Addison peered over her shoulder. "Stop." Mom shrugged, and Addison turned back to the tall man still on the other side of the door. She eased the door open and stepped aside. "Sorry it's so hot in here."

"No problem." He smiled, and Addison tried to identify his

accent, which made him even better looking than he already was. Wavy blond hair, parted in the middle, hung to the collar of his white golf shirt, which sported an emblem with the agency's logo. Logan looked more like a lifeguard than a caregiver, she thought as she eyed his chiseled arms, golden tan, and eyes as deep blue as the ocean. Her eyes cut to his left hand. No ring. There was a time in her life when Addison would have latched on to such beauty. But usually, when a single man pushing thirty looks this good, there is something wrong with him. A truckload of baggage, perhaps. Maybe a criminal record, although doubtful since he was hired out by an agency. Maybe he just wasn't a nice person. *Or gay*.

She motioned toward her mother at the table. "This is my mother, Lee Ann Burke." She paused. "Mom, this is Logan from the agency."

"Nice to meet you, Mrs. Burke."

Addison's mother finished fitting a piece of the puzzle, then stood up, and hobbled toward Addison and Logan on shaky legs, stopping a few feet short of Logan. "Addie believes that I have one foot in the grave, but not only am I not planning to check out just yet, but I'm also not old enough to be called Mrs. Burke. Please just call me Lee Ann." Mom extended her hand to Logan, and while Addison cringed at her mother's idea of an introduction, it could have gone much worse.

"Then Lee Ann it is." He smiled again, flashing a set of pearly whites, then offered Addison the file folder he was holding. "This details my credentials, and there is also a list of duties that the agency gave me, if you'd like to look over it to make sure there isn't something else you'd like me to do during my time here."

Addison looked over the paperwork. He'd been a caregiver for almost two years. Not much experience, but then Addison's mother wasn't going to require much. Logan would be more of a babysitter, as Mom had said. Addison was worried her mother's mind had suffered, and the doctor said her likelihood of having another stroke was highest over the next couple of months. Even before the stroke, Mom often forgot to take her blood pressure meds.

"It says under the list of duties that you'll be here from ten in the morning until three in the afternoon, and that's fine. But it also says that you'll prepare a home-cooked meal each day for Mom's lunch." Addison glanced up at him. "She's shaky on her legs from a recent fall, but she can make her own lunch, a sandwich or something."

Smiling again, he said, "I'm a chef, so I just offered that on my own."

Addison chewed on her bottom lip in an effort not to propose to the guy here and now. *Baggage or not.*

"Hello, I'm right here," her mother interjected. "Had a stroke. Not deaf, remember?" She cleared her throat, raising her chin a bit. Mom was an attractive woman who didn't look her sixty-two years, which was surprising considering the smoking, lack of exercise, and two stiff whiskey sours each night. Addison held her breath as she waited for her mother to go on. "Logan, I think it would be lovely if you prepared us lunch every day, and I'd be happy to pay for anything you need in the way of groceries to do so." Mom moved slowly toward the front door, looking over her shoulder once. "You kids work out the details while I have a smoke. But I wouldn't be opposed to a sponge bath, if you'd like to put that on the agenda." She giggled as the screen slammed behind her.

Addison hung her head for a few moments before she looked back up at Logan and sighed. "She's my mother. And I love her. But she's opposed to having a babysitter, as she calls it. So, I hope she doesn't give you a hard time."

"I'm sure it will be fine." He wasn't smiling anymore, and Addison wondered if he was already planning to request a transfer from the agency.

Drip, drip, drip. She tried to ignore the sound of the faucet still pounding against her temple as she dug into her purse, pulling out a business card. "This is my cell number if you need me for anything. I suspect that if you just ignore most of what she says, this should be a pretty easy gig." Addison grinned. "And she is quite capable of taking a bath on her own."

"I'm sure it will all be good. God plans the trip. I'm just the driver."

There ya go! Addison knew there had to be something wrong with this Adonis of a man. *He's a Holy Roller.*

And she didn't have room for God in her life these days. She'd trusted Him one too many times before.

CHAPTER 2

Logan cringed as he watched Addison walk to her car. *God plans the trip. I'm just the driver?* That barely made sense as a response to what Addison had said. Overkill, for sure. He wanted to seem like a responsible caregiver, someone she could trust. God was always in control, and Logan's faith had never wavered, despite the mess he was in now, but not everyone liked God shoved down their throat. He turned around when Lee Ann returned from the bathroom down the hall.

"If you'll show me where the vacuum cleaner and other supplies are, I'll start cleaning up around here." It was on the list, and Logan noticed the place could use an overhaul. Sand crunched beneath his loafers with every step he took, and as the midmorning sun cast rays on the hutch against the wall, he could see a thick layer of dust coating the top. It smelled musty too.

Lee Ann frowned. "I just cleaned this morning before you and Addison got here." She eased herself into a tan recliner and pointed to the couch. "Let's chat."

Logan glanced around again, wondering exactly what she'd cleaned and if she should even be attempting that. The woman was wobbly on her feet. "Um . . . okay." He looked at his watch before sitting down on the couch. A gold-and-green plaid couch that reminded him of a sofa his grandparents had when he was young. Just thinking about his grandmother still caused him heartache.

"Are you taking medication too?" Lee Ann grunted as she crossed one leg over the other.

"Uh, what? Medication? No, I don't—"

"I saw you looking at your watch." She raised a sculpted eyebrow.

Logan took a deep breath and forced himself to relax. He said a quick prayer, the same way he did with all his patients on the first day, asking God not to let anything happen to Lee Ann while under his care. "I guess I just feel like I need to be doing something." He smiled. "But I'm keen to chat."

She narrowed her eyebrows, frowning again. "Addison is my daughter. And I love her . . ." She paused, and Logan thought this sounded familiar. "But I don't need anyone to take care of me. I'm quite capable of getting around, taking my medication, and preparing my own meals. But when Addison first mentioned that I might need someone to stay with me, I thought that *she* might move in for a while, or at the least that she might come over every day to check on me. I was willing to play along with that scenario because . . ." She sighed, then waved a hand in the air. "Never mind. It doesn't matter. My point is, she's hired you so she doesn't have to come over every day. And the whole thing is really pointless. Does she think I might fall or a have a problem between ten in the morning and three in the afternoon, but not during the night?"

Lee Ann had a point, but Logan hoped she wasn't about to ask him to stay the nights too.

"Relax, Logan. I don't need you to stay the nights any more than I need you during the days." She chuckled. "And I can bathe myself as well." Logan felt himself blushing. "I just like to ruffle Addie's feathers sometimes. She's much too serious."

And beautiful. But Logan had to agree with Lee Ann. At first glance, Addison was eye-catching with her dark hair and eyes set against an ivory complexion with a tinge of natural color in her cheeks. But any hint of happiness was buried beneath a solemn expression. He noticed that she'd only smiled once and even that one had seemed sarcastic. Logan nodded.

"So, are you really a chef? Or did you just say that to impress my daughter?" Lee Ann was the exact opposite of her daughter. She smiled a lot.

Logan felt himself turning red again. "I'm not a certified chef, but I think I could compete with the professional blokes." He recalled the hours spent in his grandmother's kitchen.

"Where are you from? You have a lovely accent."

Logan got that a lot. He smiled. "Australia. New South Wales. But I've been here for seven years on work visas, so I like to think I sound a bit more like I belong here."

Lee Ann smiled. "Australia is on my bucket list." Her smile

faded, and she got a faraway look in her eyes before she snapped her eyes back to Logan and slapped a hand to her knee. "So these meals you will be cooking . . . American or Australian?"

"Whatever you'd like. I can grill a mean American steak, and I can also whip up some balmain bugs, although I'm guessing I won't be able to find them here."

Lee Ann shriveled up her face. "No bugs."

Logan chuckled. "They're not actually bugs, more like lobster, and they're found in the shallow waters around Australia. Fresh fish was abundant where I lived, so I can cook fish a dozen different ways. But I have a very good recipe for split pea soup. It is my grandmother's and one of my favorites."

"I love pea soup, and I can't remember the last time I had it. Too much trouble to cook for just one person, and it's not something you usually find on a menu."

"I could make the soup, and then I can make you a lamington for dessert. It's a square chocolate sponge cake with a layer of icing and coconut. It's referred to as the national cake of Australia." He paused. "Do you have any allergies? I should have asked that."

Lee Ann clapped her hands together several times. "Fun, fun. I love trying new foods, and I don't know of anything I'm allergic to." She pointed to her right. "In the kitchen, there is a pad of paper on the counter by the phone. I keep an ongoing list of things I need at the grocery store. You just put whatever you need on the list, and I'll get it."

Logan tried to recall information on the agency list, and he was pretty sure Lee Ann wasn't supposed to be driving. "Do you . . . um . . . have a ride to the market?"

She glared at him for a few seconds. "Don't you dare tell Addie I'm driving."

Logan hung his head, shaking it, before he looked back up at her. "You had a stroke, and you took a nasty fall. I don't think you should drive."

Lee Ann continued to stare at him, but she didn't say anything.

"If you will allow me to take your list with me when I leave, I can pick up what you need and bring it back tomorrow. Perhaps we can plan a menu for the rest of the week. I'm happy to make enough so that you can have dinner as well as lunch." It had been a long time since Logan had cooked for anyone.

Lee Ann folded her arms across her chest, scowling like a child.

"Otherwise, I won't cook for you." Logan grinned a little. "Will this work for you?"

She kicked her foot into motion, still staring at him. "You don't get paid to do my grocery shopping."

"Hmm . . ." He rubbed his chin. "How can we make this right?"

"By letting me drive and not telling my daughter." There was a hint of a grin on her face, but Logan was pretty sure he could close the deal and keep her off the streets.

CHAPTER 3

Addison showed up at her mother's house close to noon. Not something she planned to make a habit of, but she felt compelled to check on the new guy. As usual, the front door was open. She knocked on the slat of the screen door twice before she let herself in. She was immediately hit with the most wonderful smell coming from the kitchen.

Logan was sitting at the table with her mother, both of them with their heads down fitting pieces of the puzzle. Glancing around, she was happy to see things tidied up, and on her way to the dining room table, she ran her hand across the hutch, pulling back nothing. Even the music box her father had given her mother decades ago was shiny. *Hmm . . .*

"Addie, if you've come to check on Logan, we're doing very well, thank you." Her mother lifted her head and smiled. "Or did you come to have lunch with us? We're having split pea soup."

"G'day, Addison." Logan looked directly at her, and she

avoided his eyes for a few moments, then he drew her in like a magician with a wand. And it didn't help that his low, accented voice was also tender.

She forced herself to smile. "I can't stay for lunch, but it smells wonderful."

"Why can't you stay?" Mom looked up from the puzzle.

"I—I just can't. I work for a living, and I have appointments." She tossed long strands of hair over her shoulder, wishing she had a twisty to put her hair up. "Mom, I can't believe you're making Logan endure the heat in here, especially with the stove on. Maybe you can make an exception to your no-air-conditioning-until-July rule?"

Her mother was still rattling on about saving money on electricity when Logan stood up and walked to the window facing the beach. Addison followed him, and slowly her mother also joined them.

"I saw that man yesterday morning," her mother said as she leaned closer to the glass pane. "He was staring at my house, just like he is now. And, come to think of it, he was out there yesterday afternoon too."

"I'm sure he's harmless, Mom. Looks like he's even limping a little." Addison thought the fellow looked to be about seventy. "Maybe he's going to offer to paint your house. It needs it. I've told you I'll pay someone to do it."

"I don't need you to pay for it. I have money, but there are other things I'd like to do with it besides paint the house." Her mother kept her eyes on the man. So did Logan.

"Like what?" Addison finally asked. But Logan spoke up before her mother had a chance to answer.

"I'll go walk out there, casually, and see if I can find out what he's up to, since he's staring back at us." Logan eased around Addison and her mother. The screen door had barely slammed behind him when Addison's mom grabbed her arm.

"Is that man a gift from God or what? He looks like he stepped off of the cover of a magazine, and he can cook. And look how protective he is." She squeezed Addison's arm. "The fridge is full of ingredients to make authentic Australian food all week long."

"Mom, did you drive to the store?" Addison put a hand on her hip. "I told you that if you needed anything, I'll have someone do your shopping for you."

"Nope. Logan took care of everything. I gave him my credit card when he left yesterday, and today he showed up with everything on my list. He even bought the generic brands that I like. You always buy the name brands that are more expensive."

Addison never did anything right in her mother's eyes, so she just let the comment go. "It's not his job to shop for you, Mom."

"That's what I told him. So, we made an agreement. He does the shopping and in return, he gets two hours to help me with my puzzle."

Addison struggled not to laugh. "And he agreed to this deal? Sounds like a win-win for you. Not sure what he gets out of it."

"The boy seems to need permission to just relax. He's always nervous, moving around, and jittery. Honestly, he makes me nervous with all that activity. But he seems calm and relaxed when we're working on the puzzle or when he's cooking."

"Normally, I would tell you that it's not safe to give a stranger your credit card, but since he came through an agency, I assume he's okay. But I hope you at least got a receipt from him."

"Yes, I did. And he'd only bought himself two pairs of trousers and three shirts."

Addison's eyes opened wide, but only until her mother grinned. "Ha, ha," she said, almost smiling herself. Then she held her breath and put a hand to her ear. "Could it be? I don't hear that kitchen faucet dripping."

"Did I forget to mention that Logan fixed that yesterday before he left?" Mom grunted as she stomped one foot against the wooden floor. "Addie, if you don't at least try to get a date with that man, then there is something *wrong* with you. Not everyone will trample your heart the way Connor did. It's been almost a year since the two of you broke up, and you haven't had one single date."

"Mom, Dad's been gone two years, and you haven't gone out with anyone either." It was the only comeback Addison could think of that might fend off her mother's match-making attempts, but her mother burst out laughing.

"I'm not twenty-seven years old. And let's face it. I had thirty-six years with your father, and as you well know, it wasn't all crumpets and tea."

That's an understatement. Addison had watched her mother run her father off emotionally long before he got cancer.

Dad was probably ready to check out just to get away from her she thought, opting to keep quiet. She'd been biting her tongue a lot since her mother's stroke. In spite of everything, she couldn't bear it if anything happened to her too.

Mom put a finger against the window. "Look at that gorgeous man out there. And he seems as nice as he can be."

Addison stared as Logan talked with the man on the beach. "Guys that good-looking aren't always what they seem—I'm sure there's plenty wrong with him." She already knew of one flaw, he was the religious type. But she didn't dare get into that conversation with her mother. Addison had been raised in the church, and until her mother's stroke, Mom had attended church every Sunday. "Probably a lot of baggage too," she whispered.

Her mother wrapped an arm around her waist. "I'm going to pray that you open your heart to love again, Addie."

Addison fought to keep her eyes from welling up.

Logan had dropped his shoes on the porch. He leaned down and rolled his pants legs, sighing as the cool water lapped against his calves. When he straightened back up, he folded his arms across his chest and peered at the old man.

"You can't just stand here staring at the house like that." Logan glanced over his shoulder, glad to see that Addison and Lee Ann weren't still watching them from the window. "It makes people nervous."

"It makes *people* nervous, or it makes *you* nervous?" The old man stared toward the window again. "Yesterday was the first day I've felt well enough to walk the beach in months, to feel the warm sand between my toes, and . . ." He paused and smiled, still gazing toward the window. ". . . and to be able to see Lee Ann. Even if it's just from a distance. I don't think she's ever noticed me before. I've been walking up and down this beach and slowing down at her house for a long time, ever since I saw her sitting on the steps of her front porch." He paused again. "She waved, but that was over a year ago. I doubt she even remembers. I'm surprised that she noticed me twice yesterday and then again today." He smiled as he drew his eyes from the window back to Logan. "I'm gonna take that as a good sign. Maybe soon she'll come out here herself, instead of you." He grinned.

"I'm glad you're feeling better. I really am." Logan tucked his hair behind his ears, surprised the agency hadn't made him cut it. "But it's not safe for you and me to be hanging out together. You know that." He looked toward the window again, and in the distance, he could see Addison and her mother sitting at the dining room table. "Ronny said it's better if we stay apart, so that no one puts two and two together and figures out who we are."

"I really don't care if they do or not." The old man stormed off down the beach without looking back.

"You better care mate," Logan whispered as he watched the old man getting farther and farther away.

CHAPTER 4

A ddison decided to pay her mother and Logan a surprise visit after showing a house nearby. As usual, she tapped twice on the door, then pushed the screen open. "Mom?"

Logan appeared from down the hall, smiling. "G'day."

"Your mum isn't here. I dropped her at the beauty salon. I'll pick her up at one."

"Is everything going okay?" Addison glanced around the house before looking back at Logan. She swallowed hard and reminded herself that beautiful outside doesn't mean beautiful inside. And yet she was allowing this man to care for her mother instead of doing it herself. "Is Mom behaving?"

"Yeah, all is well." Logan tucked his hair behind his ears. His long wavy blond hair that he wore incredibly well. "I'm not finding much to do around here at the moment, and we had an early lunch. I thought I'd go take a walk on the beach before I picked up your mum. Wanna go?" He nodded toward the window, toward a surf that was higher than normal for Galveston, but she was already shaking her head.

"No. I was just in the area and decided to drop by." She took a step backward as she pulled her purse up on her shoulder, then glanced at the water again, tempted by the beautiful day, recalling the feel of the sand between her toes. She couldn't remember the last time she'd walked along the beach, something she'd probably taken for granted her entire life, but never made the time for anymore.

"I know you want to go. It's gorgeous outside." Logan smiled as he moved toward the door, kicked his loafers off, and rolled up his slacks a few times.

Please don't take your shirt off. Addison looked out the window again, deciding maybe she could learn a little bit about the man she'd selfishly hired to look after her mother. She stepped out of her heels. "Why not?" She shrugged before she leaned down and rolled up her black slacks. When she straightened up, Logan was smiling.

"Ready?" He pulled the screen door open, and Addison slid by him, inhaling a spicy scent of aftershave. They were quiet until they hit the beach and he asked which way she wanted to go. She pointed to her left and decided not to waste any time.

"How'd you end up in Galveston?" She started walking at a slow pace, and he fell in step with her. Then it hit her. The last time she'd walked on the beach was with Connor. Old memories bubbled to the surface and she was glad that there were some good ones sprinkled in with the bad ones.

"Doesn't everyone want to be in the United States?" He smiled as he tucked his hair behind his ears again. Addison pulled a hair band from her wrist and twisted her hair into a ponytail. "Windier than usual, eh?"

Addison nodded. "But why Galveston? It's a great place with lots of history right on the ocean, but I'm just curious, why here?"

"I wanted to be near the water."

Addison slowed down and lifted up on her toes when the tide swept across her ankles, realizing she hadn't rolled her pants up enough and glad she didn't have any appointments the rest of the day. Her sleeveless blue blouse was sprinkled with ocean spray as well. They picked up the pace. "So, I saw on your application that you've worked for the agency for two years. What did you do before that? Mom said you've been in the States for seven years."

Normally, there wasn't anything Logan despised more than lying, although he'd done his fair share recently. But he chose his words carefully before he spoke, in an effort to be truthful. He would just have to omit a few things. "I came here on a work visa, as an analytic consultant. An accounting job, of sorts."

Addison grinned. "You don't look like the accounting type."

"Apparently, I wasn't." Logan kept his eyes forward as he spoke. "I changed jobs several times and eventually landed an engineering job. I don't get real stoked about math, but I'm pretty good with numbers, and I like to build things."

"How in the world did you go from engineering to home

health care?" She smiled. "You don't look like the engineering type either."

He shrugged, sighed, and tried to buy himself some time,
giving a partial version of the truth. "I like taking care of
people. You have a beautiful smile." The moment he said it,
he wished he hadn't, despite his desire to change the
subject. He wasn't going to be here long enough to get
involved with anyone. As soon as he had enough money,
he'd pay Ronny to get him out of this mess. Even though
he'd been questioning Ronny's tactics since he arrived in the
United States. Logan would pray the Lord would forgive
him for what he'd done.

"Um . . . thank you."

Logan glanced her way, unsure if the color in her cheeks
was from the heat bearing down on them or if she was
embarrassed. But he decided to take advantage of her hesi-
tation and redirect the conversation. "Your mum said you
sell houses, big houses. Did you go to college for that?"

She shook her head. "When I was in high school, I had a
part-time job working for a real-estate company, and I just
sort of never left. By the time most of my friends were grad-
uating, I was making a nice living." She sighed. "And I knew
my parents couldn't afford college anyway. At least, they
couldn't ten years ago. My dad worked like a dog, but Mom
never worked. She always said it was because Dad didn't
want her to, but I'm not sure if that's true." Addison glanced
his way. "I grew up in that small house. Dad got a great deal
on it after a storm came through and the owners didn't want
to do the repairs. That was before I was born. So, Mom
doesn't have a mortgage or anything, and she's got a small
savings account, but I try to help her as much as I can."

"I sense that she'd like to spend more time with you." Logan was stepping into an area he probably shouldn't go. "She talks about you a lot."

She scowled as she slowed down and turned to face him. "I'm surprised. But don't believe everything she says."

Logan clicked his tongue as he shook his head. "If you say so, but that's a shame. It's all been good. Except . . ."

She stopped and faced him. "Except what?"

"Your mum says you're uptight, never have any fun, and don't smile enough."

Addison slammed her hands to her hips. "That's not true. I'm *fun*. I'm not *uptight*. And you saw me smile earlier."

Logan shook his head again. "Nope. I don't see it. I don't think you have any fun." He should avoid flirting with her, but she made it so easy.

She plastered a huge, fake smile across her face. "See. I'm smiling."

When Logan started to laugh, she did too, and he pointed a finger at her. "See, now you're having fun." He paused, looked into her eyes. "With me." After a few moments, he forced himself to look away and started walking again. He'd dated a few girls since being here, but none seriously. He'd avoided getting close to anyone, especially the past couple of years. He could see Addison out of the corner of his eye, watching him. There was something dangerous about this woman that made him want to know her better. And for him—that could be perilous.

Addison stepped over a jellyfish that had washed ashore, thankful she'd pulled her eyes from Logan just in time. She'd been stung three times in her life, a hazard of growing up on the beach. "That was close," she said, glancing over her shoulder. She wanted to know more about his background, how he'd gone from engineering to home health care. That seemed a big stretch. But then she saw the older man who had been staring at the house a few days ago shuffling toward them. She might not have recognized him if not for the blue baseball cap he was wearing, wisps of gray hair peeking out on either side. And he had a slight limp.

She nodded toward the man. "That's the guy who was staring at the house, the one you talked to, isn't it?"

Logan slowed his pace, then stopped. "Yeah. He's a harmless bloke. I think he just has a crush on your mum." He pulled a cell phone from his pocket, appeared to check the time, then put it back in his pocket. "Can you make it back okay? I think I'll run back toward the house so I'm not late picking up your mum. Maybe we can do this again." He winked at her and was gone.

Addison stood still as he disappeared down the beach. She didn't think it was close to one o'clock, but odd as his hasty departure was, she was pondering the wink and the earlier comment about her pretty smile. She waved at the man as he approached her and slowed down.

"Beautiful day for a walk on the beach," he said, tipping his cap as he walked by.

"Yes, it is." She took in his features. He had soft gray eyes, a pleasant smile, with teeth that might be too white to be the ones he was born with, and he had on a Dallas Cowboys T-shirt and a pair of white shorts. Addison's mother never missed a Cowboys game on television. *Hmm . . .* She spun around and jogged a few steps until she caught up with him. "May I walk with you?"

"Why, that would be lovely. Seldom does a pretty lady ask to walk with me down the beach." He smiled, and Addison smiled back at him, recalling what Logan had said.

"I saw you out in front of my mother's house the other day. You were talking to that man I was walking with. Do you know my mother, Lee Ann Burke?" Addison briefly wondered if maybe he was a stalker, but his kind eyes seemed to confirm what Logan had said, that he was harmless.

He chuckled. "I guess that young fellow musta thought I was trouble or something. But I've been walking the beach for a long time, and your mother and I have waved to each other, even though that was awhile back. I took ill, though, and just recently resumed walking." He smiled. "She probably doesn't remember seeing me, but I couldn't forget that face if I tried. I asked around until I found out who that beautiful woman was. But your father had recently died, so I knew it wouldn't be good to come calling on her." He briefly tucked his chin as he adjusted the brim of his cap. "May he rest in peace."

Addison missed and loved her father, but a man in her mother's life might be the best thing—for Addison. Logan would eventually stop coming—a thought that interrupted her train of thought—and Addison wouldn't feel the need to check on her mother as much if she had a companion.

They kept walking but the man turned to Addison. "You're as pretty as your mother."

"Thank you," she said. "I'm Addison Burke." She extended her hand, and the man latched on with a firm handshake.

"William Sparks."

Addison tapped a finger to her chin. "I wonder . . . ," she said. "Maybe you would like to meet my mother?"

He raised his eyebrows, a full smile filling his face. "I would like that very much."

As kind as this man appeared, she didn't know him, so she decided to make sure Logan was there when the introduction was made. Although, she didn't know Logan very well either.

"What about tomorrow at lunch? My mother fell recently, so we have someone coming to the house each day from ten to three; the caregiver is a chef of sorts—a huge bonus for us. I'm sure another person for lunch would be just fine. They eat around eleven."

"I think that would be lovely," he said, smiling even brighter.

Addison had never played matchmaker for her mother, and this might be a total bust. But at least she would be there to watch how it played out. And to see Logan again. The wink and compliment lingered despite the warning bells going off in her head. Not only was she unsure if she wanted to date anyone—even someone as handsome as Logan—but something wasn't quite right about him. Nothing she could put her finger on. Maybe tomorrow's lunch would help her put her finger on it.

CHAPTER 5

Logan thought he might lose his breakfast when the old man walked through the door at ten forty-five, and only seconds later, Addison pulled into the driveway.

"What are you doing here?" Logan whispered through clenched teeth, thankful Lee Ann was around the corner in the kitchen. Although, she emerged before Logan could get an answer from their guest.

"Hello, William. My daughter told me you'd be joining us for lunch." Lee Ann walked toward them at the same time Addison came through the front door. "Oh good. Everyone is here," Lee Ann said as she smiled and folded her hands in front of her. Normally, Lee Ann was in long walking shorts and a casual blouse or T-shirt. Today, she was wearing a knee length, black skirt with a tan and black blouse—and jewelry. Her dark hair was pulled into a bun, and her cheeks and lips were redder than usual.

After an awkward introduction, Logan took a deep breath and reminded himself to call the man William. Lee Ann had told him when he arrived at ten that they would be having Addison and one other person for lunch. He'd been hoping Addison wasn't bringing a date, but now he was wishing she *had* brought a significant other, instead of the man they know as William. It was easy to see that this was a romantic setup that needed to be foiled. But not only did Lee Ann dress for the occasion, the air conditioning was set at seventy-two when Logan arrived.

"Please, come and sit down at the dining room table. Logan is a wonderful cook, and today he has prepared a special dish that he learned to make from his grandmother." Lee Ann motioned to the table, already set for four. Logan had offered to bow out since Lee Ann and Addison were having a guest, but Lee Ann had told him not to be silly. *I can't believe the old man agreed to this.*

Logan walked back into the kitchen while the others sat down. He returned with a green curry chicken pie and a basket of Anzac biscuits for dessert. On his second trip, he returned with a pill bottle holding Lee Ann's morning pills that she'd forgotten to take before Logan arrived. Most days, the morning pills were still in the pillbox on the counter when he got there. Sometimes the nighttime pills were also still in there. Yesterday morning, he'd found the milk in the cabinet by the glasses instead of in the refrigerator. He'd brought a fresh gallon with him today. If Addison couldn't be with her mother, she'd been wise to hire someone.

Following a prayer, which Lee Ann always led before meals, he took time to study Addison while everyone began to fill their plates. She was in a blue pantsuit, and with her dark hair pulled into a bun like her mother's, it was impossible not to notice how much they looked alike.

27

"Logan, these biscuits are wonderful. I know you said they are for dessert, but I couldn't resist trying one now." Lee Ann passed the basket to the old man. "William, you must try these."

Logan resisted the urge to glare at *William* and instead focused on Lee Ann. "Thank you. They're an Australian staple, a sort of commemoration to the members of the Australian and New Zealand Army Corps who fought in World War I, thus the name Anzac."

William cleared his throat. "Wives used to send them to the soldiers because the biscuits would stay good for a long time since they don't have eggs in them." He smiled before taking another bite.

"Oh my," Lee Ann said. "How do you know this? Are you from Australia, too, because I certainly don't hear any accent?"

Logan held his breath as he waited for William to respond.

"No, no. But I spent a large part of my life in Australia. It's where I met my wife. It was a random encounter while vacationing there with friends." William made the sign of the cross. "God rest her soul. But I was born right here in Texas, not too far from here, Surfside Beach." He paused, frowning. "Although, there's never much surf, so I'm not sure how it got that name." Logan let out the breath he was holding and hoped that William would stop there. "Right now, I'm renting a small house down the beach from you." Glancing up at Lee Ann, Logan was sure William's eyes were twinkling, and after taking a quick look at Lee Ann, her interest seemed to match his. Logan was forcing himself to see the old man as William, repeating the name over and over in his mind so he didn't slip up.

After everyone gushed about the meal, Lee Ann excused herself to go smoke, and to Logan's surprise, William followed her. The old man despised smoking.

"Um . . ." Logan took a deep breath, choosing his words carefully. "If I didn't know better, I would say you are trying to set up your mum with that man."

Addison reached for another biscuit. "I guess you could say that." She took a dainty bite before she went on. "You said he seemed harmless and that he had a crush on my mother. And Mom needs to do something besides jigsaw puzzles all day. In fact, this is the first time I haven't seen a puzzle on the table for as long as I can remember."

Logan nodded, distracted as he was, and shoved in his last bite of chicken curry pie, glancing several times over his shoulder toward the porch where Lee Ann and her date were seated.

"Why? You don't think it's a good idea?" Addison peered across the table at him.

Logan knew it wasn't a good idea. "I—I just mean, you don't really know him. I said he *seems* harmless, but I don't know that for sure." *Lord, forgive me for the lie.* There wasn't a kinder man on the planet than their lunch guest, and Logan knew this to be a fact. Guilt wrapped around Logan so tightly that on some days, he felt like he was suffocating. At those times, he reminded himself that his lies probably saved the old man's life, and he could only hope God would look kindly on that when Logan stood before Him one day.

"That's why you're here," Addison said around a small bite of biscuit she'd just taken. "In case he came at us with an axe or something." She chuckled.

Logan enjoyed the sound of her laughter, but he wondered if she'd still see him as a good guy if she knew the truth.

Addison pushed the chicken pie around on her plate, not a huge fan of curry. *In case he came at us with an axe or something* was meant to be a joke, but as all the color drained from Logan's face, Addison stopped chewing and stared at him. "I was kidding." She paused when he didn't look at her. "About the axe."

"What?" He gave his head a quick shake before he stood up. "Oh. Yeah. I know."

Addison eased out of her chair and began helping him clear the dishes. "How's Mom? Okay?" She followed him into the kitchen and waited while he put his dishes in the sink, then she added hers. "I saw that you had to remind her to take her morning meds."

Logan leaned against the kitchen counter and stuffed his hands in his pockets, avoiding her eyes. "Yeah, she forgets sometimes."

Addison stretched her neck to the left a little, trying to meet his eyes, but his head was down as he crossed his ankles. Finally, he looked up and sighed. "I know she's not supposed to drive, so I kinda feel like I'm ratting her out, but I think she went to church Sunday. Could someone have taken her?"

"I don't know. I guess she could have found someone. How do you know she went?" Addison went to the small kitchen table in the corner and pulled out a chair.

"There was a bulletin from Moody Methodist Church on the hutch with last Sunday's date."

Addison rubbed her left temple, grateful Logan had fixed the drip, but feeling a headache coming on anyway. "Yep, that's her church. I'll ask her about it when she comes in."

"Maybe wait until after Oliver leaves so you don't embarrass her." He paused, sighing. "Hopefully, someone drove her or she'll be mad at me for telling you. But I'd feel terrible if she got in an accident and I never said anything."

Addison nodded, then sat taller. "Who's Oliver?"

Logan pulled his hands from his pockets, turned around, and started rinsing the dishes. "What?"

"You said Oliver . . . not to embarrass her in front of Oliver."

He glanced over his shoulder. "Oh, what's that guy's name?" He snapped a finger. "William. Sorry, I forgot."

Addison looked out the window, but from the kitchen she couldn't see her mother and William. "I wonder how it's going out there. They seemed to hit it off during lunch."

"I don't know. They seem to be very different people."

"Opposites attract," she said as she stood up. In the recesses of her mind, where happiness once lived, she was hoping Logan would ask her to go for another walk on the beach. It was probably a terrible idea, but the thought lingered there anyway.

"I'm Catholic, not Methodist, but I don't mind taking your mum to church. I can drop her off and pick her up while I go to Mass, or I can just attend hers as a visitor for a while. God's at both places anyway." He turned around and winked at her. Again.

"It won't kill her to miss church while she's still recovering." Addison rolled her eyes.

Logan folded his arms across his chest and grinned. "Whoa . . ."

"What?" She put her hands on her hips. "I could take her. It's just . . ." Deciding she didn't owe Logan any explanations, she bit her bottom lip, but she could feel it trembling just the same.

"I'm sorry." Logan walked toward her and touched her arm, an action that sent her pulse racing. She took a step backward, still struggling not to cry. "Addison, seriously, I'm really sorry. I was getting ready to ask what you were so mad at God about, but first of all . . . it's none of my business, and second—I shouldn't have snickered like that." He paused, sighing. "It's just . . . you sound like I used to. I was angry with God for a long time. Years, in fact."

Addison didn't want to cry. She'd done enough of that. And she didn't even know Logan. "You know what? I want to walk on the beach." She recalled Logan's comments about her not having any fun and thought about why the comment had stung so much. In high school, she'd been voted Miss Congeniality because of her 'bubbly personality.' At twenty-seven, had life already taken its toll on her and hardened her into one of those people she swore she'd never become? "Actually, I want to run down the beach. I want to get wet, play in the water, and forget about everything else for a while." She slipped out of her sandals and slid them across the kitchen floor in his direction. "You in or not?" *I'll show you fun.* It was an angry thought, this newfound need to have fun, to frolic and waste time when she should be working or doing something productive. But the beach used to represent happy times—with her father building sand castles and even with Connor. And after searching her memories, she was able to recall plenty of times that she and her mother had walked the beach looking for shells when she was a kid.

Logan grinned, and Addison knew flirting with him was a mistake, but there was such emotion and tenderness when he spoke to her about God, as if in some small way he understood what she was feeling. She had no desire to continue that conversation, but she did have a desire to find out more about him. At the very least, she couldn't help but wonder if a thread of happiness was buried beneath her grief, longing to come to the surface.

"I wish I could, but this kitchen is a wreck, and if you'll recall . . . you are paying me to take care of your mum and keep things in order."

"That's right . . . via the agency, I am your employer, and I say we go walk on the beach." In a bold move and playful —*fun*—moment she grabbed his hand and pulled him through the living room, dropping his hand to open the screen door. Her mother and William both turned her way.

"Mom, since you have company, Logan and I were thinking we'd take a walk on the beach. Is that okay? I'll help Logan clean the kitchen when we get back."

Her mother's face lit up as she put a hand to her chest. "I think that would be lovely."

Of course you do.

Addison wrestled with her emotions—about her mother, Connor, her father, and everything in between—even God. And flirting with Logan and taking a little time to play might be a nice change. But first she wanted to ask Logan something. She'd almost mentioned it earlier to her mother, but she didn't want things to get awkward for her mother in front of William. Maybe Logan would know what happened to the antique music box that had always been on the hutch, the one Addison's father had given to her mother decades ago.

CHAPTER 6

Logan had decided a long time ago that he'd never understand women, and Addison Burke was driving the point home as she skipped ahead of him down the beach, twirling around, wading through the water, and smiling more than the woman had smiled since he'd met her. Her flowing white skirt hung past her knees, and a pink short-sleeved blouse was tied at her waist. In her bare feet, with her hands in the air, she reminded Logan of a ballerina, but perhaps a dancer who'd lost her footing somewhere along the way. Whatever the reason, seeing her letting go was enticing Logan to shed a little of the anxiety he'd built up over the past couple of years, so he jogged ahead to catch up with her. But when he got close to her, she took off running. He caught up to her with little effort, but pretended it was a struggle, grabbing her around the waist to slow her down.

They went down together in the sand, landing face-to-face on their sides. They caught their breaths, and as he gazed into her eyes, he wondered what it was she was looking for. *The eyes are the mirror to the soul*, his grandmother used to say, a phrase Logan wasn't sure he understood until this moment. Inside the uptight and serious Addison, there was a playful child longing to be free. *Free of what, though?*

She propped herself up on her elbow and cradled her cheek with her hand, still facing him. As she stared at him for a few moments, he couldn't help but wonder what was about to come out of her mouth, and who would be doing the talking? Serious or playful Addison?

"If you could have one thing in the world . . . ," she began, as she pushed her sunglasses up on her head and squinted. "What would it be? I mean, even if it was somewhere you wanted to go. If you had just one wish in the entire world, what would it be?"

Logan swallowed hard, even though he didn't have to think about it. "I'd ask God to grant me one more day with my grandmother."

She stared at him, then said, "Is that something God can do?"

Logan wasn't sure he wanted to talk about his grandmother with Addison. He cherished the memories and they had become sacred to him. But Addison's eyes pierced the short distance between them in the sand, and the whole "window to the soul" thing seemed more evident than ever.

"Sometimes, in my dreams, I see her cooking in the kitchen," he said softly, found recollections dancing in his mind. "And every once in a while, she'll say, "Bub, you're gonna do great things some day. Stop worrying about me. I'm cooking with the Lord today." He paused, smiling, and tried to recall the last time he'd had the dream. "I guess that's as close as I've come to spending time with her."

"Sounds like you two were close." Addison brushed the wild strands of hair from her face. "I never knew my grandparents, on either side. My father's parents were killed in a car accident before I was even a year old, and my mother's parents weren't exactly the grandparenting type. They moved to Boston after my mom graduated from high school. I don't think she's talked to them in years." Barely smiling, she said, "When I was little, I would pretend I had regular grandparents. Silly, huh?"

Logan felt like she'd injected him with truth serum. Suddenly, he wanted to share everything, but he was wise enough to know he couldn't do that, no matter how much he wanted to. "No, I don't think it's silly. But my situation is the exact opposite. I was raised by my grandparents after my mother left me in their care, and I never knew my father. I'm not sure my mother did either."

"Did you ever see your mother?"

"Not very often. Holidays, sometimes birthdays. But when I got older, I saw less and less of her." Logan brushed loose sand from his cheek. "I never pretended like I had parents when I was little. My grandma more than made up for the fact that I didn't. She died almost ten years ago, and I still miss her."

"Will you go back to Australia?"

The fifty-million-dollar question. "One day I will." He paused. "Did you know Australia is on your mum's bucket list of places she'd like to travel?"

"No, I didn't. We're not very close. I mean, we try to be, but we just never get there."

Logan was quiet. He didn't want to pry, although he was tempted. Two older women in shorts and T-shirts went by them powerwalking, but otherwise they were alone except for some children in the distance building a sand castle. He moved to a sitting position, his knees bent, facing the water.

"I bet the beaches in Australia are beautiful, especially compared to Galveston." She pushed her lip into a pout. "I love Galveston, but we aren't known for having the prettiest beaches." She tossed her head toward the murky ocean, barely a tint of blue visible.

"It's gorgeous there." Logan fought the swelling of emotions that was almost enough to make him cry. "I'll go back someday." He just hoped that if he ever did go back that it didn't include a direct trip to jail. "There's a place I went to on the first Friday of every month when I was a kid, and I kept up the tradition as an adult. And whenever I get back, I'll keep going there. It's a place called Jervis Bay. Over the years, it got a little touristy for my taste, but the White Sands Walk from Greenfield Beach to Hyams Beach is awesome, and for whatever reason, you usually don't see more than a handful of people on the trail, unless it's a holiday weekend. It takes about an hour to make the walk."

"It sounds wonderful, but why the first Friday of every month?"

Logan recalled the first time his grandmother explained First Friday devotions, but he wasn't sure how much detail to go into with Addison. "It's kind of a Catholic thing," he finally said. ". . . to recognize the Sacred Heart of Jesus."

She was quiet and seemed to be waiting, so he went on.

"The Sacred Heart depicts Christ's physical heart as a way to symbolize his divine love for humanity." He glanced at her and saw that he hadn't lost her yet. "My grandma and I did the White Sands Walk after Mass, our idea of offering extra reparations for our sins. But after her hip surgery, it was too hard to walk that far. But I kept going."

Addison nodded, then slowly rolled onto her back and pulled her sunglasses back over her eyes, presumably to return the child to wherever she'd so briefly come from.

Addison wished she could lie in the sand, listening to the sounds of the ocean forever. And she wouldn't mind if Logan lay there with her, telling her about beautiful places across the world that she hoped to see someday. But too many things were on her mind right now. And she wasn't ready to delve into a deeper conversation about God. Just the mention of God brought a wave of emotions that she didn't understand.

She slowly stood up and brushed sand from her skirt and blouse. "Did my mother say why Australia is on her bucket list?" As Logan rose to his feet, she wondered again about the missing music box on the hutch. "I wonder what else is on her bucket list."

"Ask her." Logan faced her. "What's up with the two of you anyway?" He raised a palm to her. "You don't have to tell me if you don't want to. It's just sometimes the tension when you're both in the same room is off the charts."

Addison blew out a long breath and slowly started back down the beach in the direction they'd come from. She should have known better than to try to have a little fun. Logan probably thought her frolicking earlier was childish anyway. The situation with her mother was complicated. A topic she'd rather avoid.

"I told you before, I love my mom. She's just difficult sometimes."

Logan was quiet. Maybe he didn't agree, but he didn't know her mother the way Addison did. Logan didn't see the way her mother had treated her father before he died.

"Hey . . . uh, there was a music box on the hutch in the living room. I didn't see it earlier. Did she move it? My dad gave it to her a long time ago." She hoped it didn't sound like she was insinuating that he took it. But her inclination to trust people was miniscule these days. Connor had seen to that.

"Uh oh." Logan stopped, and Addison lowered her sunglasses and looked at him over the rims. Slowly, he eased his own shades lower until they were eye to eye.

"Uh oh, *what*? Did it break? If you broke it, it's okay. Accidents happen."

They continued to look at each other for a moment before he pushed his glasses back up. Addison did the same.

"I had no idea it was a gift from your father. I made a comment the other day that it was a beautiful music box. She asked me if I thought it was worth anything, and I told her I had no idea." He took a deep breath. "She asked me if

I'd take it down to the pawn shop on the Strand and see what I could get for it. So, I did."

Addison dug her toes in the sand and clenched her fist. "Why would she do that?"

"I don't know."

She let out a lungful of air, closed her eyes, and tried to steady her breathing. "How much did you get?"

She waited, and when he didn't answer, she asked again. "How much did you get for the music box my father lovingly gave to my mother, a gift she obviously felt no sentimental attachment to?"

Logan hung his head. "Forty dollars."

Addison began to tremble, despite the heat, and she wondered if Logan was telling the truth. "You have got to be kidding me."

"Nope." He looked up at her. "I'm really sorry. I just figured she was short on cash. I asked her why she didn't sell it on eBay or put it on Craigslist. I told her she'd probably get more, but she said she'd already tried."

Addison's jaw dropped. "She'd already tried *what*?"

"She said she'd already tried to sell it on both those sites."

Addison burst out laughing. "Uh, hardly. Mom barely knows how to email, so I doubt she'd know how to use either of those sites."

Logan hung his head again. "I'm starting to feel like a go-between for you and your mum. Addison, you need to talk

41

to her and find out what's going on. But I can tell you this . . . she's been selling tons of stuff online just since I started. Several times I've taken things to the post office for her on the way home."

"Has she ever said why?" Addison unintentionally grunted after the question, which wasn't very ladylike, but she didn't care right now. "Is she that short on money?"

Logan took his glasses off, rubbed his eyes, then put them back on. "Again, I think you need to talk to her. We haven't discussed her financial status, and I certainly wouldn't inquire about such personal stuff. But . . ." Logan sighed.

"Oh no. What else? Just tell me." Addison took a deep breath and held it.

"Yesterday, she told me she listed her car for sale." He paused, but quickly added, "but maybe she thinks she won't be able to ever drive again."

Addison shook her head. "I never told her that. The doctor just suggested that she not drive for a month or two just as a precaution in case she were to have another stroke, which usually happens not long after the first one. But I would never have told her to sell her car."

Logan turned his head and stared down the beach and away from Addison. She tapped him on the arm. "Is she selling anything else I should know about?"

"You need to talk to her, Addison." Logan kept his gaze down the shoreline.

"I will." They started walking again, faster this time. After a while, she said, "So . . . she's selling tons of stuff. Like what else?"

Logan stared straight ahead. "Pretty much everything."

CHAPTER 7

Addison waited for her mother to say goodbye to William, then she told Logan he could leave early for the day.

"Um, what about all the dishes in the kitchen? And—"

Addison waved him off. "It's fine. I'll take care of it. I need to spend some time with my mother."

Logan looked with sad eyes back and forth between Addison and her mother, as if he were being marched to the guillotine. Then he motioned for William to follow him out the door.

"That was rude, Addie." Her mother grimaced as she slipped out of a pair of tan sandals—which even sported a bit of a heel—that Addison didn't recall ever having seen. "I was enjoying William's company, and it's not your place to dictate visiting hours around here. This is *my* home. And good grief, what happened to you? You look like you've been rolling around in the sand." Mom grinned. "Were you and Logan rolling around in the sand?"

Addison looked down at her clothes, then chose a spot on the floor to sit down, leaning against the recliner. She stretched her legs out in front of her and crossed her ankles, waiting for her mother to get comfortable on the couch.

"Mother . . ." Addison rubbed her temples as she tried to steady her breathing.

"Well, I must be in trouble if you're calling me *Mother* instead of Mom."

"Did you pawn the music box dad gave you, the one on the hutch?" Addison nodded toward the piece of furniture that had been in that same spot her entire life, along with the framed seashell picture hanging above it.

"No. I asked Logan to pawn it." Her mother spoke softly, hesitantly, as she cringed a little. "Why?"

Addison drew in a deep breath before looking at her again. "Did that music box not have any sentimental value for you? Did you even take into consideration that Dad worked hard to buy you gifts?" She slapped a hand against the rug on the floor next to her. "And why are you selling everything?"

Her mother stiffened. "Addie, this might come as a surprise to you, but I don't have to run things by you. What I do with my things and my money is my business. And if this is about you paying for a babysitter for me, I never asked or wanted you to do that."

"Mom . . ."Addison lifted herself into the chair, knowing she'd leave a wet spot but not caring. "I know you don't have to tell me your business, but Logan said he thinks you are selling everything you own!" She flung her hands in the air, dropping them in her lap. "Why would you do that? Where are you going to live? Are you broke? You should have talked to me about this. I mean, even your car?"

Her mother tapped a finger to her chin, but was quiet for a few moments. "I'm going to travel."

Addison's eyes grew larger. "Like, uh . . . for the rest of your life? So much traveling that you need to sell all your possessions?"

Mom raised her chin. "I won't need these things where I'm going."

Addison slouched into the chair and put her finger to her temple again, thankful that the air conditioner was running, but knowing a migraine was coming. "Where are you going?"

"Anywhere I want."

Addison wished her father were alive right now. "So, to make sure I understand . . . you're going to sell everything, pocket the money, and travel the world? For how long? Until your money runs out? Then what? You'll expect me to support you?"

Despite harboring resentments toward her mother, Addison rarely showed any outward disrespect, and her mother's hurt shone across her face and her eyes watered. But it was still a question Addison wanted answered.

"Addie . . ." Mom blinked a few times. "I'm well aware that you make a tremendous amount of money for your age, a fact that I'm not always sure is in your best interest. But rest assured, I will never ask you to support me. I have money set aside for my travels. The reason I am selling everything I own is so that I can move into an assisted living facility.

"A year ago, I would have thought I was much too young to consider something like this, but if I'm not too young to have a stroke, then I suppose I'm not too young to have someone nearby if I needed help. The facility is furnished, so I don't need all this stuff." She waved her arm around the room as if the things she'd collected her entire lifetime were nothing more than petty trinkets.

Addison tried to decipher what was happening. "So, you're selling the house too?"

Her mother sat even taller as she folded her hands in her lap. "Yes. And don't worry, you can have the listing."

Addison considered telling her mother that this house was small potatoes compared to what she was used to, but the sting of her mother's slap still lingered on her heart. "Do you think that's all I care about, the listing?"

Her mother's glare felt like a burn against Addison's skin. "No. I think you also worry that I'm being foolish with my money and that I'll become a financial burden to you, but I assure you my affairs are in order."

"Mom, calm down. I've never thought you'd be a financial burden, and even if you were, I would have helped you."

Her mother propped her elbows on her knees, folded her hands, and rested her chin on them as she leaned forward. "Addie, I don't need or want your financial help. All I've ever wanted is for us to be close and to have the type of mother-daughter relationship that seems to have eluded us over the years."

This was a conversation Addison had avoided for years, but maybe it was time to confront the elephant in the room. "Mom, I love you. But it was very hard for me to watch the way you treated Dad, especially when he was dying."

"Your father had a roof over his head and food to eat. He never missed a doctor's appointment, and I made sure that he took all of his medications. I gave him a sponge bath daily when it became necessary and shaved his face. And when he became too weak to wipe his own butt, I did that too. So, maybe you need to elaborate."

Addison swallowed back the lump in her throat, wishing she'd avoided having this inevitable conversation. "What about tenderness? What about love? You acted like you were his nurse or caregiver, but where was an ounce of compassion? And I don't mean just when he was sick! For as long as I can remember, Dad was nothing but loving and kind to you, and you gave him nothing resembling love in return!" *There. I said it.* Addison waited for relief to wash over her, but instead dread filled her every pore. Would this be the last straw, the one that pushed Addison and her mother so far apart that they'd never find their way back to each other? She waited for her mother to burst into tears, but instead, Lee Ann Burke stood up and pointed a finger an inch from Addison's face.

"Is this what the chip on your shoulder has been about? How I treated your father? The fact that I didn't toss his butt out on the street should be calculated into that bottle of bitterness you've been hauling around. But I'm tired of protecting him, for your sake or his. Your father was a lying cheat . . . and everyone around here knew it but you. I stayed humiliated for most of our marriage! And I know you think I was lazy and never wanted to work, but your father was insistent I be a good little housewife, and I think that was largely because he didn't want me frequenting any of the places he might be if I had a job in town. Places I might see him flaunting one of his many girlfriends. Oh, the affairs came and went. And the apologies were stacked on top of each other like the worthless words they were. Eventually, someone new always came along." Her mother fell onto the couch, and her face was so red that Addison feared she might have another stroke or worse. She sat quietly, wanting to find reasons for how this couldn't be true. Her mother could be a lot of things, but a liar wasn't one of them.

"Why didn't you leave him?" Addison still wasn't sure she believed these accusations, but as she pondered her mother's statements, flashbacks of her childhood came forth like a wrecking ball, one in particular. Elementary school—it was open house. Her mother excused herself to go to the restroom, and Addison's young teacher was showing her father Addison's latest artwork. She'd only been a kid, but something about her father's exchange with the teacher had left Addie feeling unsettled, though she didn't understand it at the time.

"I should have left him, Addie. I know that now." Her mother reached for a tissue on the end table and dabbed at her eyes. "But marriage is a sacrament, something I was totally committed to, and in my mind, it was best for you to grow up with two parents under the same roof."

"Why are you telling me this now?" Addison fought the tremble in her bottom lip.

Her mother offered the slightest hint of a smile, then whispered, "Because you asked."

49

~

Logan paced the small living room in the old man's house. He'd reprimanded him all the way home.

"Quit pacing, Logan. Just sit down and relax."

Logan shook his head. "You're unbelievable. I shouldn't even be here, at your house. You know what Ronny said, that our chances of getting caught are highest when we're together. And you're going to blow it for both of us by playing kissy-face with the woman I work for."

"Well, there's been no kissing, but I'm hopeful." The old man grinned.

"This isn't funny. If you don't want to spend the rest of your life in jail, you'd better take this seriously."

The old man pounded a fist against the coffee table. "I'm tired of all this. I'd rather go to the authorities and do my time in jail if I have to. I can't keep up this charade. I finally have a chance with Lee Ann, and you're trying to make me give up the one thing that gives me hope. Can't an old man hold on to a shred of happiness?"

Logan sat on the couch next to him, compassion and fear all wound up in a tight ball in his stomach. "Maybe it's the price we paid to keep you alive."

The old man turned to him, tears in his eyes. "This isn't living. This is existing."

Logan leaned back against the couch, and both of them stared straight ahead. He knew the old man's comments were true. Much of the time, Logan felt like he wasn't living either. He was always looking over his shoulder. "If we see this through until Ronny can get things worked out, then—"

"Ronny, Ronny, Ronny. I'm sick of hearing what Ronny's gonna do!" The old man's arms flailed above his head. "We're in this mess because of Ronny. We should have just faced the music two years ago. It wouldn't have been near as bad as facing prison. I'd rather go to prison for the rest of my life than feel like I'm always on the run."

"What about me? Do you want me to spend the rest of my life in prison too?"

The old man turned toward him. "It's not like we murdered anyone, ya know? Maybe we do our time for what we've done, then get on with our lives the way the Lord intended us to, without a bucketful of lies strapped to our backs." The man sighed. "Don't get me wrong. I'll forever be grateful to you for what you did for me. You saved my life. But this just isn't living."

Logan stared at the elderly man's watery eyes, feeling his own eyes tear up, then said, "I just need a little more time and money, then I promise I'll get us out of this mess. Please, Grandpa. Just trust me."

CHAPTER 8

Addison pushed all the pictures from her bed with one sweep of her arm, sending them flying in every direction in her bedroom. Then she walked around and stomped on each one. The photos with Connor's face staring up at her, she ground those beneath her heel. It was one of those things that a girl would never want to go public with, but a ritual that gave her a level of satisfaction just the same.

When she was done, she flung herself onto the bed and cried. But this time, she wasn't just wallowing in her own self-pity, but crying for her mother as well. She glanced at her phone on the table by her bed; she hadn't talked to her mom in four days. Addison was curious if her mother had fired Logan since he'd spilled Mom's secrets. But she hadn't been curious enough to call and find out. She'd missed two calls from her mother, but she was still sorting things out in her mind.

She wasn't sure what upset her more, that her father had done this to her and her mother for years, or that her mother hadn't told her. She decided that she was more upset with her father. *Men cheat.*

Fifteen minutes later, she was dressed and out the door. By the time she arrived at her mother's house, she still didn't know what she was going to say. She pulled the screen open and tapped on the wooden door, a sure indictor that the air conditioning was running.

Her mother answered the door wearing a modest white sundress and flat white sandals. "Well, this is a surprise." She stepped back so Addison could enter, then closed the door behind her. "I wasn't going to drive if that's what you're worried about."

"Then how were you going to get to church? I wasn't even sure you still had a car." Addison fought to keep the tremble from her voice. "You look very pretty." She blinked her eyes a few times to push back the tears pooling in the corners.

Her mother put a gentle hand on each of Addison's arms. "Addie, sweetheart . . . I just never told you because you idolized your father. I didn't want to take that from you."

Addison didn't try to stop the tear that slid down her cheek. "You should have told me. All this time, I've been awful, blaming you for everything that went wrong between you and Dad."

Mom smiled. "And it was a burden I was willing to carry if it kept you from any further upset. But maybe I was wrong."

Addison opened her mouth to speak, but nothing would come out. She wanted to tell her mother she was sorry, but a knock on the door took her away from her thoughts. "Who's here?"

"Logan. He offered to take me to church. He's a little late. We were supposed to run a couple of errands on the way to church." She shook her head, but grinned. "If that boy has one fault, it's that he's always running behind." Mom's grin spread into a full smile. "But it's a fault I'm willing to overlook, and today . . . it worked out for the best." She pulled the door open. "Hi, sweetie. Come on in."

Addison frowned. *Sweetie?* But then her eyes fixated on Logan with his gorgeous blond hair neatly groomed, and he was wearing black slacks, a dark blue shirt, and a tie. Addison glanced down at her blue jeans, heeled sandals, and short-sleeved red blouse, feeling underdressed, but relieved she wouldn't have to take her mother to church.

"Addie came to take me to church." Mom folded her hands in front of her, and it was impossible not to hear the joy in her voice.

"No, no. I didn't want her to drive herself." She rolled her eyes, but smiled. "But since you're here, I'll let you two go." She eased around Logan, but he caught her by the arm.

"Why don't we all go?" Logan dropped his hand, but raised an eyebrow.

Addison shook her head. "No, that's okay. Church isn't really my thing." She glanced at her mother, who hung her head, then Addison looked back at Logan. "But you two go."

"Addie, it's Logan's day off, and I'm sure he'd rather go to his own church." Her mother sighed. "Wouldn't you, Logan?"

Logan opened the door, pushed the screen open, and in a firm voice said, "I'm taking the two prettiest ladies in town to church, then out to eat at Shrimp 'N Stuff."

Mom clapped her hands. "How wonderful. I haven't eaten there in a long time, and it's one of my favorite places on the island."

Addison hadn't been to Shrimp 'N Stuff in years either. It was a super casual, cheap place for seafood, and not somewhere she frequented. But they served some of the best seafood in Galveston. Her mouth watered just thinking about it. *How bad could one hour of church be?*

Logan followed Lee Ann down the aisle of the church, Addison lagging far behind. He figured she'd make a run for it any minute. Her face was white earlier when they approached the door. He glanced over his shoulder to make sure she was still coming, and she was. Shuffling slowly down the aisle.

"How long's it been since she's been to church?" Logan asked Lee Ann as they eased their way into an aisle.

"A long time," Lee Ann said as Addison caught up to them.

After a few minutes of silence, Logan whispered to Addison. "Don't look so scared. I promise you'll come out of this in one piece."

She glanced at him, and barely offered up a weak smile. "I'm only here for the fish later."

Prior to the service starting, Logan prayed about the choices he'd made recently and once again, he asked God to forgive him for the lies, and to guide him back to a place where he could live an honest life. Then he prayed for continued good health for his grandfather.

He glanced at Addison. She didn't appear to be breathing. Logan could clearly recall a time—not that long ago—when he fell away from God. When the Lord wouldn't heal his grandfather. His grandmother had passed, and the thought of losing the other most important person in his life had been overwhelming, especially because Logan had prayed and prayed for God to heal the old man. But instead of healing his grandfather, God had shown Logan another path. And his grandfather had gotten better. But now it took every ounce of faith Logan had to trust God to guide his journey. Logan feared there must have been a fork in the road somewhere, because it sure felt like he'd taken a wrong turn.

He cleared his thoughts so he could focus on the service, and even though it was quite different from the Catholic Mass he was used to, he could feel the Holy Spirit moving him, and when he heard Addison sniffle, he cut his eyes in her direction without moving his head. Her eyes were filled with tears, and Logan had no way to know if they were happy or sad tears. Church had a way of doing that to a person, especially if you hadn't been in a while. Without giving it much thought, he found her hand and grasped it in his. She squeezed back, but kept her eyes straight ahead. It was an odd moment. Logan didn't know her very well, but as he held her hand, he felt like he could feel her pain, and he had an overwhelming desire to fix whatever ailed her. Logan's grandmother had told him since he was a young boy, that he was a fixer. At times it had been more of a curse than a blessing—the ends he would go to in an effort to "fix" a person or situation.

Addison abruptly let go of his hand, eased out of the pew, and hurried down the aisle. Logan looked at Lee Ann as a pained expression fell across her face, and he stepped out of the pew to go after Addison.

~

Mistake, mistake, mistake. Addison rushed out the door and into the Texas heat, breathing in the smell of the ocean, and hoping her mother or Logan didn't come looking for her. But when she heard the large, wooden church door close behind her, she turned to see Logan standing on the steps.

"I'm fine. I just needed some air." She waved a hand toward him. "I'll be back in a minute." Dabbing at her eyes with her finger, she turned away from him, but she could hear footsteps getting closer, until he was close enough to inhale the spicy scent of his cologne. He gently put his hands on her shoulders.

"What's wrong?" he asked in a whisper, the feel of his breath sending a shiver down her spine.

"I don't know." It was the only answer she had. "I feel so stupid." She turned to face him, and the tenderness that shone in his expression melted her resolve, and when he pulled her into a hug, she laid her head against his chest. "Who cries in church?" Right now, she just wanted to stay in the comfort of his arms, a man she barely knew.

Logan eased her away, moved strands of loose hair from her face, then dabbed at a tear on her cheek. "I think that sometimes, when we've been away from God for a while, we're overwhelmed by the way He welcomes us back with pure love and forgiveness. The Lord's heart is always open and welcoming to us, even if we've turned our backs on Him."

She hung her head, then looked up at him. "I went through a bad breakup, and my dad died, all at the same time. It was just too much, and I prayed and prayed and prayed for peace, for comfort . . . and nothing. I just kept sinking into a bottomless pit of despair. So, I threw myself into my work, and I stopped talking to God. How can I get past that?" She paused, sighed. "And do I even want to? God let me down at a time when I needed Him most. What if He does it again?"

Logan cupped her cheeks in his hands, a slight smile playing on his beautiful face. "God doesn't let us down. He gives us choices, free will. It's up to us whether or not we choose the path He's chosen for us. And much of the time, we veer off on our own journey, which never leads us to true happiness. But it's the struggles that bring us back to God and closer to Him than we were before."

"So, we need to go do a bunch of bad stuff or make poor choices, then God will reel us in and make it all better?" She paused, holding up one finger, even though Logan was still close enough to kiss her, a distracting but lovely thought. "Why do we even have to go through the bad? Why can't He just lead us to the good? Connor cheated on me, and I was devastated that my dad died." She sighed. "I'll always love my father, but apparently he didn't do my mother right either, and now I'm eaten up with regret about the way I've treated my mom the past few years." She paused. "And I'm furious with my father."

"Anger and regret will feed on you like a hungry predator, leaving you raw and unable to forgive yourself. Believe me, I know."

Something about Logan's voice made her sense he was

facing his own demons. "I can't just stand here and make a conscious decision that I'm going to start praying again, that I want God back in my life."

Logan's face broke out into a big smile. "Sure you can. It's that easy."

She stared into his eyes, longing for his lips to just gently brush against hers, which seemed wrong in light of the subject matter and the fact that they were ten feet from the church. She eased herself away, putting an arm's length between them.

"Do you trust God?" she asked in a shaky voice.

"I do." He looked away from her, his gaze set to his left. "I disappoint Him over and over again. I make bad choices, step off the right path, and all the while God is there to lead me back to Him." His eyes brimmed with tenderness when he looked back at her. "And right now, that's exactly what I'm doing. I'm waiting. I'm waiting for answers. I'm waiting for him to tell me what to do, to tell me how I can get home."

Addison held her breath as Logan's eyes watered up. More was going on with Logan than he was admitting. "Home to Australia?" she finally asked.

"Home to *Him*." He paused. "And yes. Home to Australia."

She swallowed hard, and as he stepped closer to her, warning bells sounded all over the place. *He wants to go home. Don't get close to him.* "Just get on a plane and go home," she whispered as he grew even closer.

"I wish it was that simple."

She waited for him to kiss her, knowing she'd let him, but he took a step back and held out his hand to her. "Maybe we should both go back in. And instead of praying for ourselves, why don't we pray for each other?"

Addison liked that idea. Something about Logan screamed out to her that he needed prayers, and praying for someone else was within her comfort zone today. "Okay," she said softly.

She took his hand and together they walked back into the church, and when he squeezed her hand, she squeezed back again.

What's happening?

With me and God?

And . . . with me and Logan?

CHAPTER 9

Logan was in dangerous territory. Not only had church and Shrimp 'N Stuff become a regular Sunday outing for Logan, Lee Ann, and Addison—but Logan's grandpa had started attended the Methodist church with them too. One big happy family.

It was bad enough that Logan and his grandfather were spending time together, something Ronny had said to avoid, but Logan was starting to have some fairly serious feelings for Addison. He'd stopped himself from kissing her several times. He loved watching her spiritual journey and the healing relationship developing between Addison and her mother. But everything else had disaster written all over it.

He knocked on his grandfather's door after work one day.

"Good, I'm glad you're here." Grandpa shuffled toward him in a pair of gray sweatpants and his Cowboys T-shirt. "What do you think?" He winked. "It's not real. You think she'll be able to tell?"

Logan's heart rate tripled. "Surely that isn't what I think it is."

"Of course it is. I'm going to make an honest woman out of Lee Ann."

Logan glared at his grandfather, glanced at the ring, then back at the crazy old man. "She doesn't even know your real name. How can you possibly think about proposing? Not to mention you've only been hanging out with her for a few weeks!"

"The heart knows what the heart wants, and my heart wants Lee Ann Burke. So quit yelling." The old man slammed the ring box shut and huffed as he walked off.

Logan fell into his grandfather's recliner, covered his eyes with one hand, and slouched into the worn leather. "I gave Ronny the money to buy back our lives, so to speak. We're going home."

"I'm not going anywhere without Lee Ann."

Under different circumstances, Logan would have been thrilled that his grandfather had found love again. "Do you really think she will marry you when she finds out the truth?"

"I know she will. It's that kind of love." His grandfather sat down beside him. "I'm a blessed man, Logan. I told Lee Ann I love her, and she told me she loves me too. The Lord is giving me another shot at happiness."

"Grandpa . . . listen to me. You're going to be marrying her in a jail cell if we don't handle this the right way. Can you please just sit tight until I figure out what to do?"

"I don't like that Ronny fellow. I don't think he's steered us right from the beginning." Grandpa pointed a crooked finger at Logan. "Something's not right."

"There are a lot of things that aren't right. Where do you want me to start?"

Addison stared at the place where the television used to be. "I can't believe you sold your TV too." She glanced around the empty house as she slung her purse on the couch; the only piece of furniture left. Most everything was gone or packed in boxes. She'd been to breakfast with her mother and didn't have any appointments today, so she'd been lingering around until Logan showed up. This morning her mother had tripped walking into the café, and later confessed she'd forgotten to take her nighttime meds again.

"They have a television at the assisted living facility, but . . ." Mom grinned, and Addison felt like she and her mother had reached an entirely new level in their relationship, more like girlfriends. Addison had a couple of girls she hung out with from time to time, but most of them were married and had husbands and children. ". . . but I think William is going to propose."

Addison stopped breathing for a few moments. "What? Are you kidding?"

Her mother reached for both of Addison's hands and squeezed. "I love him, Addison. I really do. Would you approve?"

Addison's eyes filled with tears. "I can't think of anyone

who deserves to be loved and happy more than you." She fell into her mother's arms and thanked God that her mother was finding some joy in her life. Praying had become a part of her routine. She didn't know if God was answering her prayers, but she was practicing patience, like Logan said. *Logan. A force to be reckoned with.* Some days she thought he might be madly in love with her, and other times he seemed to avoid her like the plague.

"Maybe I'm wrong, Addie, but he's hinted about marriage a couple of times."

"I'm happy for you, Mom, but you haven't been seeing him for very long."

"The heart wants what the heart wants, as William would say. And Addie . . ." Her mother shook her head. "We're not getting any younger, and William has almost ten years on me."

"I hear you."

Mom cleared her throat. "So. What about you and Logan? William and I can see the spark between you two."

Addison shook her head. "No. It's not like that with us." *I wish it were.*

"For someone whose nature seems so laid back, that boy has a nervousness about him that makes it hard for him to relax."

Addison knew exactly what her mother was referring to. She'd start to feel that things were moving in a more romantic direction with Logan, then he'd look over his shoulder, or seem to remember something he'd forgotten, and he'd back off. "Maybe he doesn't like me . . . enough." *And can I trust him not to break my heart?*

"Hosh posh! That's silly. I catch the guy staring at you all the time."

Addison smiled. She'd caught Logan gazing at her more than once, and it always sent a warm wave over her. "Well, he sure doesn't act on it."

"Logan hasn't dated anyone seriously in over two years. He shared that with me recently when I tried to discreetly pry into his personal life." Mom cupped her chin with her hand. "I didn't get a sense that he was recovering from a broken heart or anything. But I know he's trying to save money, so that might be part of his hesitancy." She paused as her expression fell flat. "Uh oh. I know what it is."

Addison straightened on the couch. "What? And how do you know so much about Logan anyway?"

"You are paying that agency good money for him to spend a lot of time with me. We have lots of time to talk."

Addison had considered cancelling the agency service, but she was terrified she might not see Logan again. "You said you know what it is that's holding Logan back. What is it?"

"You already know what it is. He wants to get home to Australia. That's a long way to carry on a long-distance relationship. I think he is protecting his heart. And protecting yours too."

Addison shrugged. She'd considered that possibility. And despite her growing feelings for Logan, she'd felt herself holding back for those same reasons.

"But just remember . . . the heart wants what the heart wants." Her mother pulled her into another hug.

Addison swallowed back a knot in her throat. Again. How could she have not seen the beautiful and deserving woman her mother was? Addison's anger with her father wasn't going to go away over night, and Logan had said that if she forgave her father, it would give her peace. She was trying.

"I hear a car pulling in. Must be Logan." Addison pulled a compact out of her purse and checked her lipstick.

"So, that's why you've been loitering. You were just waiting for Logan." Her mother giggled, but didn't move from her spot next to Addison on the couch. "He lets himself in."

Addison tossed the compact back in her purse, but glanced at her mother when Logan knocked. "He's probably not walking in because he sees my car out there."

They both lifted themselves from the couch and moved toward the door.

"I'm so glad you've been running the air conditioner," Addison said, shaking her head. "That's why no one ever visited you before."

"Really? Because I think there were other reasons you didn't spend much time here as well." She slapped Addison on the butt as if she were a small child.

"Hey," she said, jumping as her mother opened the door.

A heavyset, middle-aged woman with salt-and-pepper hair was standing on the other side of the screen.

Addison's mother spoke first. "Can I help you?"

"I'm Evelyn. The agency sent me."

"No, no, no," her mother said, wagging a finger at the woman. "Logan has been coming since the beginning, and I really don't want to train someone new."

"Mrs. Burke, I've got many years of experience, so please don't worry." The woman pointed to a file folder she was holding. "Would you like to see my references?"

"Um . . . no, dear. Just go back to the agency and tell them to send Logan." Mom nodded and was about to close the door when the woman cleared her throat.

"Mrs. Burke, the man who was coming here doesn't work there anymore."

Her mother brought a hand to her chest. "Of course he does. There's some confusion somewhere."

Evelyn shook her head. "No, ma'am. I'm sure. They specifically said I am replacing someone who got fired."

Her mother lightly stomped her foot. "This is ridiculous, but I'll get it straightened out. I don't need anyone here today anyway. My daughter is here." She nodded to Addison. "Bye, now."

After Addison's mother slammed the door in the woman's face, she walked to the phone. "I'll call the agency." She dialed the number while Addison wondered how Logan could have gotten fired. *Maybe for always being late?*

"A recording picked up," her mother said as she put the cordless phone back in the receiver. "I don't have time to wait for the next available associate." Mom paced back and forth a few steps. "I can't imagine why Logan would have been fired." She picked up the phone again and dialed. "I think we should just go to the agency, but I need to call William first. He mentioned coming over here, so I need to let him know we're leaving."

A moment later, her mother set the phone in the holder, the color having drained from her face.

"Mom, what is it?" Addison moved toward her.

"I—I don't know. That's odd." Her mother blinked her eyes a few times. "A recording said William's phone number has been disconnected. What do you think that means?"

Addison took a deep breath. "I don't know. Maybe he didn't pay the bill. But right now, I think we should head to the agency. Maybe leave William a note on the door, in case he shows up."

They both picked up their purses from the couch and headed out.

Addison had a sick feeling in the pit of her stomach.

CHAPTER 10

Addison held tightly to her mother's hand as they sat facing the administrator of the home health care facility, a woman her mom had gone to school with. Addison was too stunned to offer much comfort to her mother.

"Let me get this straight." Addison finally said. "Both Logan and William outstayed their visas and were deported? And William is Logan's grandfather?"

The woman on the other side of the desk—Nancy—nodded. "Apparently, they came here so that William could participate in a cancer trial being offered. William thought he had dual citizenship. He was born in Texas, but married in Australia. Logan came here on a five-year work visa. But just as they were preparing to head back to Australia, William had a relapse, so they didn't leave when they were supposed to. So, Logan had outstayed his visa, and there was a problem with William's paperwork with regard to dual citizenship." Nancy hung her head, sighing, before she looked at Addison's mother. "Lee Ann, I could get in big trouble by telling you all this. And I'm not even sure I'm explaining it all correctly. There was another man involved that seemed to have lead them astray and encouraged them to sign some things they shouldn't have. He was their sponsor to come here."

Addison's mom waved Nancy off, and Addison didn't know which question to start with, but at least they weren't deported because they'd committed some horrible crime. She squeezed her mother's hand. "See, Mom, it isn't so bad."

Her mother let go of Addison's hand and dabbed at her face with a tissue Nancy had given her. "If William has dual citizenship, why did he have to leave?"

Nancy leaned back in her chair, slipped off a pair of reading glasses, and sighed again. "I don't know all the details about William's status, just that there was a problem with his paperwork. But I'm afraid there's more, Lee Ann."

Addison's heart flipped in her chest. "What else?"

Nancy spoke with a kind, sympathetic voice. "We all really liked Logan, so this is sad news for us as well. Logan and William had paid someone to establish fake identities, so that William could be treated for his cancer when he relapsed, instead of taking a chance that they might be deported. They'd started out in Houston, but that's how they ended up in Galveston, at UTMB, for treatment. There was another cancer trial specifically for the type of cancer William had at UTMB. They were both facing jail time, but from what I've been told, the judge was lenient in light of the circumstances. He told them they could both go home to Australia, but they'd never be permitted back in the United States."

Addison's mother sobbed quietly to herself as Addison fought her own tears. Then it hit her. "Fake identities? Who are they, then? If they aren't Logan and William?"

Nancy leaned forward in her chair. "I don't know who they are. I had to pry the information out of the person who brought us the news. But the woman wouldn't tell me their real names."

"No, no, no." Her mother spoke loudly. "Are you telling me that you don't know what William's real name is? How will I get in touch with him? Is William cancer-free?"

"I'm sorry, Lee Ann. That's all I know. And I had to really push hard to find out that much." Nancy stood up, an indicator that their time together was ending. The woman had bags underneath her eyes, and Addison suspected this had been quite an ordeal for the agency as well. Her mother darted out of the room, and Addison lifted herself from the chair, reached across the desk, and shook Nancy's hand.

"I need to go take care of my mother. Thank you for telling us this much."

"Good luck. I can tell Lee Ann is heartbroken."

Addison sighed, nodded, and left Nancy's office, knowing she needed to be strong for her mother, even though her own heart was broken. She found her mother standing outside near an ashtray, just staring down at it. It was then that Addison realized that she hadn't seen her mother smoking lately.

"You know, I quit smoking for that man." Mom sniffled,

raising her eyes to Addison's. "I felt like I had something to live for."

Addison blinked her eyes a few times. "I'm so sorry, Mom. So, so sorry."

"I don't even know his name!" She stomped a foot, then raised her eyes to heaven. "Why is God doing this to me? Don't I deserve some happiness?"

Addison wanted to tell her mother that God works in ways they don't understand. If she'd learned anything at all from Logan and her times in church, it was that each person had their own individual relationship with God, and as with all relationships, sometimes there was conflict. Her mother would have to work through this in her own way. Addison recognized having the thought, but also knew that she was struggling with what had happened as well, questioning how God could give her and her mother a glimpse of happiness, only to snatch it away. Then she remembered something.

"Mom. I think William's name might be Oliver."

Her mother's eyes grew round. "Oliver? He doesn't look like an Oliver. He looks like a William."

Addison shrugged. "Maybe, but I heard Logan—or whatever his name is—accidentally refer to him as Oliver."

Mom grabbed Addison's arm. "Do you know his last name?"

"No. I'm sorry. You're going to just have to wait to hear from him."

"What if I don't?"

Addison could kick William—Oliver—for hurting her

mother like this. "Then it wasn't meant to be," she said softly. Her mother started walking to the car, and Addison slowly followed.

~

Jack climbed out of bed in possibly the most bittersweet moment in his life. He'd never been happier to be home in Australia, but his heart hurt, wondering what Addison and Lee Ann must be thinking. Such a betrayal, even if it had all been in an effort to save his grandfather's life.

"Jackson, I made dippy eggs with vegemite soldiers for breakfast," Grandpa hollered from the kitchen.

It should have been music to his ears, to know that an Australian breakfast was being prepared by his grandfather in their own kitchen, but Jack wasn't sure he could stomach much of anything.

"You're a chipper mate this morning," he said to his grandfather when he walked into the kitchen.

"Can't cry over spilled milk," the old man said. "Just gotta clean up the mess an refill the cup." He placed a plate in front of Jack. "Besides, I have a letter all ready to put in the mail to Lee Ann."

"Why don't you just call her?" Jack pulled the soldier toast from the dippy eggs and took a bite.

His grandfather sat down with his own plate. "If she's going to reject me, I'd rather read it in a letter. Besides, writing a letter is a chance to really tell her how I feel."

"You do understand that you can't ever go back to the

United States, right?" Jack took a sip of coffee the old man had brought him.

"I know." He blew out a breath of frustration. "All that dual citizenship stuff took place fifty years ago. I have no idea if I did it wrong or what happened, and that Ronny fellow didn't help our cause. But there's nothing keeping Lee Ann from coming here."

Jack grunted. "Nothing but a mound of lies and betrayals."

"Jackson . . ." Only Jack's grandparents had ever called him that, and despite the situation, he welcomed hearing it again now that they were home. It was familiar. "I am alive and cancer-free. I'm not in jail. And I am in my own kitchen. So, I praise God for these things. My life is never going to be complete without Lee Ann, though." He paused, scratched his chin. "Are you going to contact Addison?"

Jack should his head.

"Why? I know you care for that girl."

Jack had spent the past three days in and out of a time warp of jet lag, his thoughts jumbled, his heart hurting. But in the end, he'd made a decision. "Addison had a bad breakup with her last boyfriend. The guy cheated on her. And she just recently found out some things about her father. More betrayals. And now me. You're right. I do care about her." *I think I'm in love with her.* "But we weren't around each other long enough for me to make a lasting impression on her, Grandpa. I feel like it's kinder to let her go."

His grandpa finished chewing a piece of toast. "But did she make a lasting impression on *you?*"

"It doesn't matter. Addison is more rigid than her mother,

and I don't see forgiveness coming easily to her about this." He set the toast down. "I feel like I need some time out of my head."

"Last time you said that, you headed to Spain and walked five hundred miles."

Jack recalled his pilgrimage, the Camino de Santiago. It had been one of the most rewarding spiritual journeys of his life. When he closed his eyes, he could still recall laying eyes on what was believed to be the shrine of the apostle St. James the Great in the Cathedral of Santiago de Compostela. He was lost in memories when his grandfather spoke up again.

"Well, at least we have money again."

Jack forced himself to scoop up another bite of dippy eggs with his toast, even though he wasn't sure it was going to stay down. "I know. I messed up."

Grandpa chuckled. "Yeah, we weren't very good criminals. We should have thought to transfer funds before we decided to change our names."

They ate in silence for a while, then his grandpa burst out laughing again. "If I marry Lee Ann, Addison will be your stepsister. If things had worked out with you and Addison, would she have been your wife and stepsister? Would she have been my stepdaughter or daughter-in-law?" Still smiling, he tapped a finger to his chin. "Will you be Lee Ann's son-in-law or stepson?"

Jack shook his head, grinning, as he pushed his food around on his plate, thinking what an odd and wonderful problem that would have been. But he forced the thought aside and tried to focus on his next move. "I think I'll go get a haircut."

His grandfather put his fork down and stared at him. "So . . . you really are thinking of taking off?" When Jack didn't answer, the old man said, "Because you always get a haircut before you go off on one of your sabbaticals."

Jack tucked long strands of hair behind his ears. "Maybe."

CHAPTER 11

Addison hurried through her last appointment for the day, anxious to check on her mother. Mom didn't want to hire anyone else through the agency, and Addison had gone along with that, even though she was worried about her mother remembering to take her meds . . . and worried about her overall mental state.

"Look, look, look!" Mom jumped up and down like a toddler when Addison walked into the living room. "Read it. It's from Wil—I mean Oliver." She smiled as she pushed an envelope at Addison. "I'm going to have to get used to that, calling him Oliver. Read it."

Addison was glad to see her mother so happy, but cautious about sharing her mother's joy until she heard what *Oliver* had to say. And even then, she wasn't sure if she wanted her mother involved with someone like him. She pulled the letter from the envelope.

My Dearest Lee Ann,

I don't know what you've been told about my departure, but let me just say this—I've had four great loves in my life. The Lord, my beloved wife Claire, my grandson Jackson (Logan) . . . and now you. Yes, there were lies and betrayals. But please know that I wasn't lying when I said I love you.

Addison took a deep breath. *Jackson. His name is Jackson.* She kept reading.

Perhaps I shouldn't make excuses for what we did, but I guess I will anyway. I had cancer, Lee Ann, and while I was prepared to meet my Maker, I wasn't sure Jackson could handle another loss. He loved his grandmother very much. Claire and I raised Jackson (we're the only ones who call him that, others just call him Jack). He's a good boy. Or, I guess I should say, he is a good man. Although, I look at the man he's become, and it's mindboggling where all the time went.

I was in the United States (yes, I really was born in Surfside Beach, Texas) for cancer treatment. Things got complicated, and well . . . next thing you know, we were both being sent back to Australia. And I've been told we can't go back to the United States.

I'm asking you from the bottom of my heart to forgive this old man. I've enclosed a voucher for a round-trip ticket to Australia. Or just make it one way—that's what I'll be hoping for. My boy tells me our homeland is on your bucket list, anyway. Come to the Australian Outback and let an old guy show you around. He'd be willing to love you till the end of time if you'd have him. Have I mentioned that I love you?

Addison couldn't help but smile, but she wondered how he could afford such a gift since she'd gotten the impression that neither Logan—Jack—or Oliver had much money. She glanced at her mother, whose face glowed like a new bride, blissfully happy and hopeful for the future. Addison knew her mother had forgiven Oliver before she even read the letter.

I'm happy to purchase a ticket for Addison to accompany you here if you are uncomfortable traveling by yourself. I'd be happy to do this, and of course, I'd be delighted to see her as well.

Addison swallowed back the sob that threatened to escape, determined not to ruin this moment for her mother. But not even a mention about Jack, if he missed her or thought about her, or anything. Maybe she'd misread the unspoken signals between them. Or maybe that's why he'd never kissed her.

So, my love, I'm including my phone number at the end of this letter, in hopes to hear your voice soon. If not, I'll understand. But just know, I don't have any regrets. If things had turned out any differently, I wouldn't have been led to you.

My love always,

Oliver Lloyd Easten

Addison fought the disappointment that cocooned her, an ending that never really had a defined beginning. But what did she expect? She handed the letter back to her mother.

"I'm happy for you, Mom. I really am." She smiled, genuinely, as it warmed her heart to see such joy from her mother. "You deserve this, and I guess I don't even have to ask if you're going."

Her mother grabbed both her hands, still clutching tightly to the letter. "Come with me, Addie."

Addison shook her head. "No, Mom. I wasn't invited."

"Of course you were! Didn't you read the part about Oliver getting you a ticket too?"

Addison sighed. "No, Mom. That's not what I mean. Jack didn't invite me, and I haven't heard from him. It would be awkward to just show up. If he wanted to see me, he would have called or written. Clearly, his feelings for me weren't the same as Oliver's are for you." She hugged her mom, then eased away. "I am very happy for you, if not a bit worried. How well do you know this man? Well enough to fly across the world to visit him?"

Her mother cupped her cheeks. "Yes, and you're going to have to trust on me this. And I'm going. I've already called him, and I'm leaving Thursday. We're old, Addie." Mom clapped her hands together. "No time to waste."

Addison knew her eyes were bulging. "Already? I mean, that's in three days. Don't you have to get things in order, pack, take care of things? What about a passport?"

Mom waved an arm around the empty room. "I've done everything. I got a passport months ago when I knew I would be traveling someday. And if I choose to come back, I already have a reserved spot at the assisted living facility. But Addie . . . I'm not ready to just be an old lady who travels from time to time. I want to *live*, to be loved."

"You will call me every step of the way, right? And you'll remember to take your meds too, right?"

Mom nodded, grinning. "And I won't talk to strangers either."

Addison smiled, as her mother brought two hands and the

letter she was still clutching to her chest. "Addie, this letter just came today. Have you been home yet?"

Addison shook her head. "I came straight from my last showing. Why?"

Mom turned her around and almost pushed her out the door. "Scoot! You might have a letter waiting at your house too!"

"I doubt it." But suddenly, she was anxious to get home.

Jack listened as his grandfather detailed Lee Ann's travel plans for Thursday. "I'm happy for you, Grandpa. I really am." He wished more than anything that Addison was coming, but his grandfather had offered to buy her a ticket, and there'd been no interest on her end. He was pretty sure he'd misread her.

"I still think you should phone Addison. It's not too late."

Jack slouched into the couch and crossed an ankle over his knee and shrugged.

"You haven't gotten a haircut yet, so you must not be ready to hit the road." His grandfather chuckled.

"I have an appointment to get it cut this afternoon."

"Then what?" Grandpa folded his arms across his chest.

"I don't know yet."

His grandfather sat down beside him. "Take some time to get out of your head, as you put it. You've certainly got the money to do so since we couldn't get to our money for two years. I'm proud of the way you worked so hard in the States to take care of both of us when things got so messed up and you could no longer be Jackson Easten the accountant or engineer. I know home health care wasn't your career choice."

Jack shrugged. "It wasn't so bad. I met a lot of nice people. Besides, it was all Logan Northrupp was qualified to do."

Maybe when you get back, you'll decide to go back into accounting or engineering. Although, I gotta say, neither of those seemed suited to you. Maybe go to culinary school! The world is wide open to you, Jackson. Choose your path, and if it feels right, it's the right one."

Jack nodded. Even though he wasn't sure anything was going to feel right without Addison.

Addison didn't even shut the car door as she darted to the mailbox in front of her house. She yanked the lid down, grabbed the mail, and rushed through the three envelopes. Not a one of them from Jack. Tucking the mail under her arm, she stopped at her car to get her purse, slammed the door shut, and marched to her front door. She turned the key in the lock, but heard someone honking, so she glanced over her shoulder and gasped.

Connor? She stood perfectly still as he swaggered toward her never looking better in a pair of khaki shorts and a yellow Polo shirt. His dark hair was neatly parted to one side, and he was sporting a dark tan to go with the new Corvette he'd apparently bought since they'd broken up.

"Nice car," she said softly, glancing around him at the black Vette. "What are you doing here?" She quickly calculated that she hadn't laid eyes on him in almost eight months, and that had been a chance meeting at Starbucks. An awkward moment with him and Mandy . . . the girl he'd cheated with, glued to his side, blinking long, fake eyelashes at Addison.

He kept walking until he was right in front of her. "Mandy and I broke up." He hung his head, then looked back up at her. "And it's just as well. She knows I've always been in love with you."

Addison stared at him "Who ended it? You or her?"

"She did. But Addison—" He reached for her arm and she pulled away.

"I'm not your consolation prize, Connor. I'm no one's second choice."

"Baby, you've always been my first choice. Always." His eyes watered up as he moved closer again, but Addison put an arm out.

"No, Connor. You can't come here just because your heart has been trampled on, then expect me to welcome you back with open arms. It doesn't work like that."

"I know that. I'm just asking for another chance. Doesn't a guy deserve a second chance?"

Addison lowered her arm and stared at the man she'd been ready to marry, to build a life with. And here he was, offering to make that dream a reality.

"You cheated on me. For months."

He hung his head again, and a tear rolled down his cheek. "I know. And I've never been sorrier. Please, babe. Let's give it another try."

At that very moment, Addison knew that she should feel some sort of hope for the future. But the only thing that came to her mind was Logan. *Jack.* She searched her mind in an effort to recall one conversation that she'd ever had with Connor about God, faith, love, loss, or anything that wasn't a shallow conversation about the materialistic things they both wanted down the line. Jack probably didn't have a dime to his name, but he'd shown her the way back to God and guided her onto a path of spirituality. She liked where she was in that regard.

But as she recalled the fond memories of Jack, she reminded herself that he hadn't tried to contact her in any way. She was easy to find on the Internet via the company she worked for, Facebook, and several other public profiles. She'd never even shared a kiss with Jack. And yet, with Connor, she'd planned an entire future, lending weight to the fact that maybe Connor did deserve another chance.

"I'll think about it," she finally said to Connor.

"I'll spend the rest of my life making this up to you, Addison. I swear." He moved closer, but again, she kept him at arm's distance.

"I said, I'll think about it."

He took an exaggerated step backward, nodding. "That's all I can ask." He kept walking backward until he was at his car. "I'll call you later."

"Okay," she said and she watched him drive down the

street, keeping her eyes on his car until he was around the corner and out of sight.

Later, after a shower, she spread the familiar pile of pictures on her bed, but for the first time in a year, she didn't feel like throwing them on the floor and stomping on them. She picked up each photo, recalling where they had been when the picture was taken, soaking in some of the happiest memories of her life.

By the time the phone rang later that evening . . . Addison had made her decision.

CHAPTER 12

J ack was thankful that he and his grandfather lived close enough to Jervis Bay to walk there. He needed to get an early start before the weekenders started arriving and the winds picked up in the afternoon. He made his way to the Greenfield Beach picnic area, south of Vincentia, to start the White Sands Walk. As he looked out over deep blue water, he dug his toes into what was recognized by the Guinness Book of Records as the whitest sand in the world. A far cry from the beaches on Galveston Island. But he felt like he'd left a part of himself back in Texas.

As he hugged the water's edge, he pulled his phone from his pocket. Addison's number had been easy enough to find, but every time he opened her contact page on the phone, he hit End. So, instead, he'd just stare at the picture that he'd attached to her profile, a photo from the real estate agency's website. Was it real, what he'd felt for her? And did she feel anything for him? He'd intentionally avoided kissing her, and even though he regretted it on one level, he was relieved on another level, unsure if his heart could have taken the separation.

He'd been in love one other time in his life, right before he'd left for the United States. There'd been all kinds of promises made, but the distance between continents had not made their hearts grow fonder.

He picked up the pace and hoped he'd spot a kangaroo today. Or maybe a dolphin. Either way, his trek would take him through a chain of pristine beaches, through the bush track, and some of the most gorgeous rock formations on the planet. A good place to clear a guy's head. His backpack was in the car, and once he'd stabilized his thoughts, he'd figure out which way to head. He was just glad to be out of the house before Lee Ann arrived, due there any minute. And it was an opportunity to visit his favorite place in the world.

Addison stood beside her mother, in awe of her surroundings. Oliver and Jack's house wasn't right on the beach, but you could see the ocean from the wraparound porch that enclosed the entire house, which was painted a light shade of blue and set against white stone. Calburra Beach, population 3,500, looked like the setting for a postcard. Oliver had shared with her mother that a trusted friend had paid the bills and kept the place up while Oliver and Jack were in the United States.

"I'm so glad you decided to come with me at the last minute." Mom was glowing like a schoolgirl on her first date with two large red suitcases beside her. Addison had packed so hurriedly, she only had a carry-on, and she was sure she'd forgotten some things. Not to mention, she had gotten a look at herself in the mirror at the airport bathroom and she was far from glowing. She'd never been one to sleep much on a plane, and jet lag hung beneath her eyes in dark circles. She glanced again at her mother and didn't think she'd ever looked more beautiful.

Her mother knocked on the door with shaky hands. Oliver had insisted on picking them up at the airport, despite the fact that he would have to reschedule a doctor's appointment. But Mom had argued that he needed to keep the appointment and that she and Addison would take a cab. Addison's mother had won that argument, and Addison suspected Oliver would give in to her mother's every whim. She'd been concerned about the recent hiccups in his life and if her mother would be okay here, but seeing her mother this happy made it seem worth any risk.

"I just assumed . . . that they . . . lived modestly." Addison glanced around at the pristine houses, exquisite flowers and greenery, and shops in the distance. Touristy, but quaint. "They're rich."

"I wouldn't care if Oliver lived in a hut," her mother said, a permanent smile fixed on her face. And in reality, Addison had been prepared to stay in a homestead of modest means, and she hadn't cared either if it was a hut. But the thought of spending the night under the same roof as Jack caused her heart to skip a beat. The four of them had spent so much time together over the past few weeks, it would almost seem like a reunion, but she wondered how Jack would react when he saw her.

Addison had shown up at the airport with hopes she could

get a ticket on her mother's flight. She'd packed, met Connor for coffee, given him the news that there would be no second chance for them, them zoomed to the airport. She knew she'd never forget the look on her mother's face when Addison came down the aisle of the plane. And if things didn't go well with Jack, there would be no regrets. It was a mother-daughter trip—and this was a second chance she wasn't going to miss.

As the breeze swirled around them on Oliver and Jack's porch, the door finally opened. Oliver blinked his eyes a few times. "You are early. A gift from God." He rushed into Lee Ann's arms, and Addison knew she was blushing as the couple smothered each other in kisses right there on the porch. She tried to look past Oliver, to see if Jack was lingering behind him, but all she saw was a wide open space decorated with colorful wicker furniture, brightly lit, and a bird chirping in the background.

"That's Heidi our budgie, similar to what you'd call a parakeet," Oliver said as he eased away from Lee Ann, then moved toward Addison. "What a wonderful surprise. But shame on you for not allowing me to buy you a ticket." He kissed Addison on the cheek before pulling her into a hug.

"It was a last minute decision," Addison said, still trying to see over his shoulder in hopes that Jack was home.

"Come in, come in. Jack prepared some appetizers before he left, and I have tea or coffee ready."

Mom began to question Oliver about his doctor's visit, but all Addison heard was *before he left*. Of course, he would be at work. Why hadn't she thought of that? But would he have a job so soon? Maybe he was running errands. Most likely, he wanted to give his grandfather and Addison's mother time alone, so he'd made himself scarce for a while, since he didn't know Addison was coming. Or would he have made himself scarce had he known she was coming? Finally, she couldn't stand it anymore.

"Is Jack here?" she asked above their conversation.

Oliver let out a heavy sigh, and Addison's stomach flipped as she swallowed hard.

"My dear Addison. I wish we would have known you were coming. Jack is a responsible, loving grandson. But from time to time he ventures off the beaten path to clear his head. And this time, I think perhaps his heart was involved." Oliver touched her gently on the arm. "I'm afraid Jack left about an hour ago."

"Oh." She forced a smile. "Will he be back soon?" Suddenly, she was more anxious than ever to tell him how she felt. She'd wasted too much time in her life wishing it away. She was going to live her life, like her mother planned to do. And the first thing on the agenda was to tell Jack how she felt. If he rejected her, she'd treat this as a nice vacation, then go home. Maybe it was all the kissy-face she'd witnessed with her mother and Oliver, but the moment she saw Jack, she was going to smother him in affection too.

"I don't know when Jack will be back, Addison."

Oliver's words stung like a hundred bees. "Um . . . what?"

"Sit down." He motioned them to a colorful couch that faced a plush garden on the other side of a plate glass window. Heidi was enjoying the sunshine from a large cage on the patio, vocalizing the intrusion. Once they were seated, Oliver went on. "I might not hear from Jack for days or even weeks. From time to time, Jack ventures out on a bit of a spiritual journey. Although . . ." He tapped a finger to his chin. "I think there is probably surfing involved."

Addison tried to smile, unsuccessfully. She'd been right, though, pegging him as a lifeguard or someone with a love of the water, with his golden tan, strong arms, and long blond hair.

"Anyway, whenever I do hear from him, he will be devastated that he missed you. I think that's part of the reason he went to 'get out of his head' as he calls it. I think it's his heart he's trying to run from. And we all know there's no escaping our feelings."

Addison's emotions merged. "Feelings for me?" she said in a meek voice, hoping she hadn't misunderstood.

Oliver smiled. "Of course, dear girl. The boy is in love with you. But he is convinced you could never forgive him for the lies." He glanced at Lee Ann. "I've been on bended knee daily, thanking God that you chose to forgive me." He reached for her hand before turning back to Addison. "How long can you stay?"

Addison took in the image of her mother and Oliver, possibly the cutest couple she'd ever seen. "I don't know for sure."

"I have the guest bedroom ready for your mother, and I could have the other extra bedroom down the hall ready with little effort. I'd just have to clear some of Jack's painting supplies out of there. He's really very good. I've encouraged him to show some of his work at a local gallery, but he says it's just a hobby."

"I had no idea he painted." Addison realized she didn't know much at all about Jack. Maybe this trip hadn't been a good idea. As she eyed her mother and Oliver, she could see that the girl trip part of this adventure was coming to an end.

"I'll probably just wander around and see some of the nearby sights, then go home in a few days. But don't go to any extra trouble, I can stay in Mom's room with her."

"Absolutely." Mom smiled at Addison, but Addison could see her own hurt reflected in her mother's eyes. "We will have a wonderful time while you're here. And maybe Jack will check in during that time."

"Maybe," she whispered, swallowing back tears.

Jack wiped sweat from his forehead, thankful he'd cut his hair. Even if he did look like an engineer now, a job he'd get to someday, just not anytime soon. When the time was right, he'd design his own home near Jervis Beach, with a view of the ocean. Only thing that would be missing would be Addison. He wondered if he'd made a mistake by not calling her, and he tried to envision the Addison he'd left, the one who'd become more trusting, the girl who smiled more. The woman who'd reestablished her relationship with God. He pulled his phone from his pocket, pulled off his sunglasses, and pulled up her profile again. What did he have to lose? *Just call her.* But he stuffed the phone back in his pocket, knowing he'd given her another reason not to trust the men in her life.

When he reached the entrance to the White Sands Walk,

he chugged some water, put his shades back on, and prepared to walk the hour-long loop down the bush track to Hyams Beach. It would be his best chance to spot a kangaroo or some of the more colorful birds in the area. He'd keep his hand on his phone in case a photo op presented itself, but he also needed to give some thought to where he might go after this. He was about three hours south of Sydney, but the big city had no allure for him. Getting out of his head required reliance on God, the beauty of his surroundings, and mental clarity. When he got home, he'd make some plans to put together a life for himself. He slowed his pace to take time for prayer.

Addison decided to give her mother and Oliver some time alone. She suspected they had a future to plan. Addison tried to envision her mother living here, so far away. But she was resolved to support whatever choices her mother made.

When she reached the beach, she slipped off her flip-flops and tucked them in the pocket of her white cargo shorts, thankful for the loose pink shirt she'd chosen. Her outfit reminded her of her day at the beach with Logan. *Jack, Jack, Jack.* She was still getting use to that. *Jack Easten.* She'd been wearing pink and white that day too.

She was sure this was the whitest sand she'd ever seen, and she'd known the water would outshine Galveston by a mile, but it was even bluer than she could have imagined. Watching two sailboats in the distance, she wondered if she'd have a job when she got back. She'd been there for a long time, but her boss hadn't taken kindly to her giving one-day notice that she was leaving and no firm date of when she'd be back. She was missing three closings this week that would fall on Sandra. But something deep inside of her knew that she'd never have peace until she found out if there was something real going on with her and Jack. It felt genuine to her, but she reminded herself that he hadn't made contact.

When she saw the entrance to the White Sands Walk to Hyams Beach, she recalled Jack's comment about going there the first Friday of each month. She stopped in her tracks, the wind tossing her hair across her face. She'd realized on the plane that today was the first Friday of the month. A sign from God or a coincidence?

She stood perfectly still, staring at the sign to the entrance. Oliver had made Jack's trip sound more like a sabbatical, not a trek in familiar territory not far from where he lived. But she did want to see the place Jack found special enough to walk it once a month for most of his life, minus the past seven years.

She made the turn on the trail, and within a few minutes, she could see the allure and thanked God for leading her to this place. She could almost feel Jack nearby, and it was easy to picture him getting lost in thought amidst the soothing coos from nearby birds, mixed with a gentle breeze. Taking her time to absorb her surroundings and chat with God, she rounded the corner . . . and had the shock of her life.

Standing in front her, tall and fierce, was a huge kangaroo. And as he moved toward her, it become clear . . . this large fellow was not happy.

CHAPTER 13

J ack ran a hand through his much shorter hair and wondered if Addison would like it this length. Was this how it would always be? Constant thoughts about the Texas girl he'd been forced to leave behind. He rounded the corner, and at first glance, he was excited to get his wish. A kangaroo with his back to him was farther down the trail. But when he got closer, he could see a woman in the distance. He hoped it was a local who knew what to do when facing a kangaroo, and not a tourist.

He picked up his pace, and right away, he knew the woman wasn't from here. She was taking steps backward away from the kangaroo. Locals knew to turn to the side and avoid eye contact. A kangaroo that size could slice open a person's abdomen with its sharp claws. One kick could crush a person's insides. It was rare to see one this time of day. Normally, you'd only catch a glimpse of a buck this size in the early morning hours or twilight.

"Hey!" Jack called out to try to get the animal's attention. He'd bet money that the woman had food in her pockets.

Otherwise, a buck like that would have just taken off. But the tourists had made a habit of trying to feed the kangaroos, despite the warnings, and the animals had become more comfortable getting close to people. "Hey!" he yelled again as he got closer. "If you have any food in your pocket, toss it to the side!" He tried to peek around the animal to see if she heard, but all he saw was something fly to her left. *Must have been food.* The animal scurried toward the tossed item, then hopped away.

Jack put a hand to his forehead as he drew closer, and what he saw almost dropped him to his knees.

"Addison . . ." He could barely speak as his heart thudded in his chest. He glanced around, then back at her, to make sure she was real.

Addison smiled, tempted to run into his arms like she'd envisioned, but the thought that he'd never called or written returned to the forefront of her mind like a roadblock she couldn't get past. "Hi Lo—*Jack.*"

His jaw hung low as he slowly walked toward her. She hadn't recognized him at first with his short haircut. "What are you doing here?" A smile filled his face as he stopped a foot from her.

"Someone who frequents this place saved me from a big kangaroo that wanted my energy bar." She shrugged, trying to look casual. "First Friday of the month. I took a chance." Forcing a smile, she trembled, despite the heat swirling in the breeze. "Nice haircut."

Jack was still smiling. "What are you doing here?" he asked again. "Grandpa said he offered to buy you a ticket, but he said you weren't coming."

"It was a last-minute decision." She was tempted to tell him that she didn't want her mother traveling alone, but that wouldn't be true, and one thing she wanted above all else right now was honesty. "I wanted to see you," she said almost in a whisper.

"On a normal First Friday, I would have already walked this loop. I was late leaving today. I helped Grandpa make some snacks to have for your mum when she got here." He paused, shook his head. "What are the chances that I'd run into you before I took off on my trip?"

She took a deep breath and reminded herself that she couldn't expect Jack to change plans he'd made just because she showed up. But at the very least, she wanted to know how things stood. "Where are you headed?"

He laughed. "I have no idea!" His expression grew serious. "I guess I was running . . . anywhere . . . somewhere, to clear my head and see if it would help my heart." He gently pounded his chest with one fist.

"What—what's the problem with you heart?"

He hung his head for a few moments before he looked back up at her and locked eyes. "There's this girl . . . woman." He waited for a reaction, but Addison wasn't breathing. "She is what's wrong with my heart. I was falling for her while I was pretending to be someone else. But I can't help but wonder if she has similar feelings for me."

"Ah . . . so you lied to her," she said, keeping her eyes on his.

"I did. My intentions were good, but I was pretty sure this woman wouldn't forgive me for the lies. The last two men in her life that she was close to betrayed her, and I didn't think she'd see past my lies to understand why I did what I did."

She pressed her lips together, trying to play it straight and cool, but all she could focus on was Jack saying he'd fallen for her. "What if—what if . . . this woman understood your motives, but she didn't understand why you didn't call or write."

Jack latched onto both her shoulders. "I would tell her that I didn't want to cause her more pain. I've missed you, Addison, and I don't think it's a coincidence that you're here. I thought I saw something in your eyes, too, something real, and I—"

She cupped his cheek in her hand, leaned up, and pressed her mouth to his, lingering there for a long while. She was pretty sure she heard angels singing in the distance. When she finally eased away from him, what she saw was a kind man, someone who loved his grandfather, and who had been very good to her mother. A man who'd shown Addison a way back to God.

"Now, we've kissed," she whispered. "What now?"

Jack let out a long breath. Would he leave on his sabbatical? Would she hear from him again? What did the future hold with Jack in Australia and her life in the United States?

"We don't have to figure everything out this very minute." He pushed a strand of hair from her face. "But . . . I need to know . . . need to know if . . ." He sighed. "I regret the way I've handled things, and I'm having trouble forgiving myself for lying to you. To God. I just need to know if—"

"If I have feelings for you?"

He nodded, keeping his gaze on hers. "Yes. I'll accept whatever answer you give me. I just need to know."

She latched on to his hand and gently pulled. "Let's take a walk." He squeezed her hand, and she squeezed back. "Someone once told me that regrets will feed on you like a hungry predator, leaving you raw and unable to forgive yourself."

They were quiet for a while. Only the birds were having a conversation. But she figured she'd kept him on the line long enough. She slowed down, turned to him, and said, "My feelings for you are real. Real enough to come all the way here to see how you felt about me."

He wrapped his arms around her, kissed her on the forehead, and held her tightly. She held her head against his chest, against the beat of his heart, and wondered what the future held. Especially, the next few minutes. Would he still feel the need to leave, or was he done running?

After a few moments, they started walking again, but Addison couldn't shake the feeling that Jack had more on his mind. At the next inlet, the beach came into view, and he guided her off the path, and once they were in the sand, they moved toward the water. At the water's edge, Jack turned to her.

"Addison, I can't ask you to give up your life."

She choked back the knot forming in her throat and wondered if this was the part where he told her he was still leaving. He sat down in the sand, and she did the same, deciding to avoid his comment, afraid she might cry.

"This is the prettiest beach I've ever seen." She stared out at the deepest part of the ocean, where the royal blue met with the horizon. "I bet you're glad to be back here."

He stared out at the water for a few moments, then twisted to face her. "The tides have turned, and we live on different continents now, but I want you in my life." He reached for her hand, and she smiled.

"Tides ebb and flow," she said softly. "Like life. Like relationships. But the lowest ebb is the turn of the tide, as Henry Wadsworth Longfellow would say."

"I believe this is a tide worth turning." Jack leaned over and kissed her.

Addison waited.

"How long can you stay?" He reached for her hand.

How long do you want me to stay? She shrugged, unsure how to answer. "I—I don't know."

He smiled, and Addison was tempted to say *forever*.

"You up for a road trip?" Still smiling, he squeezed her hand.

"To where?" Not that it mattered.

Now it was Jack who shrugged. "Wherever the tide takes us."

Addison had never done anything in her life that hadn't been meticulously planned out. She wasn't even sure she'd brought the basics for this trip. And now, Jack wanted her to pick up and just leave, destination unknown. Yet, nothing had ever sounded better to her. God had lead her this far. She smiled and squeezed his hand.

"I think I'm long overdue for a road trip."

And when Jack's lips met hers, she knew that she'd reached the place she wanted to be. With Jack.

RECIPES

Logan's Anzac Biscuits

- 2 cups rolled oats
- 1 cup all-purpose flour
- ⅔ cup caster (superfine) sugar
- ¾ cup desiccated coconut
- ⅓ cup golden syrup
- 125g (4.5 oz.) unsalted butter
- 1 teaspoon bicarbonate of (baking) soda
- 2 tablespoons hot water

Preheat oven to 325°. Place the oats, flour, sugar and coconut in a bowl and mix to combine. Place the golden syrup and butter in a saucepan over low heat and cook, stirring, until melted. Combine the bicarbonate of soda with the water and add to the butter mixture. Pour into the oat mixture and mix well to combine. Place tablespoons of the mixture onto baking trays lined with non-stick baking paper and flatten to 7cm rounds, allowing room to spread. Bake for 8–10 minutes or until deep golden. Allow to cool on baking trays for 5 minutes before transferring to wire racks to cool completely. Makes 35.

Logan's Split Pea Soup

2 cups dried, green split peas

7 cups water

1 tsp. canola oil

2 cups cooked ham, cubed

2 cups carrots, chopped

1 cup onion, chopped

1 cup celery, chopped

1 cup potatoes, peeled and diced

1 t. salt

½ teaspoon garlic powder

½ teaspoon pepper

¼ cup minced fresh parsley

In a large pot, bring the peas, oil, and water to a boil. Reduce heat; cover and simmer for two hours, stirring occasionally. Add the next eight ingredients; cover and simmer for 30 minutes or until vegetables are tender. Stir in parsley. Makes 10 servings.

READING GROUP GUIDE

1. Logan (Jack) willingly broke the law in his effort to save his grandfather. Do you feel he was justified in doing so, or would you have done things differently? If things had not played out exactly as they did, Logan and William (Oliver) probably wouldn't have met Lee Ann and Addison. Was that God's plan all along?

2. Was it right for Lee Ann not to tell Addison the truth about her father? Lee Ann was trying to protect Addison, but by doing so, their mother/daughter relationship suffered. What do you think would have happened if Lee Ann had been honest with Addison about her father's infidelities?

3. Addison took a leap of faith when she decided to go to Australia, hoping Logan had feelings for her. Have you ever done anything like that, or known someone who has? What were the results?

4. If there is a sequel to this story, what would you want to happen?

BONUS SHORT STORY — CHRISTMAS BY THE SEA

Galveston, Texas . . .

Parker squeezed his eyes closed, the pain in his left leg unbearable, but it was the rising water that slung his mortality around like a slingshot with no aim. Murky flood-waters swirled and collided in organized unison atop his chest. Another three or four inches and the water would be up to his chin.

As rain pelted against his face like rounds of ammunition, Parker gasped for breath in shallow gulps, his faith teeter-ing. He'd been a good Christian his entire life, but as he faced death now, fear and apprehension ruled. Had he really lived as good a life as he could have?

He tried again to move his trapped leg, only to cry out into a weather event that had no mercy, a tropical storm turned hurricane within the past few hours. His sales meeting had run long, and he wondered if his coworkers and friends had managed to get off the island safely. After his car stalled near the cruise terminal, he'd tried to wade to higher ground, but branches and dead tree limbs shared the water with him, and now he was lodged against a concrete pillar, held firmly by a tree branch that crushed his leg in a way that left it feeling numb and detached from his body.

Is this how I will go, God? As a lifelong resident of Galveston Island, the Texas Gulf Coast was as familiar to Parker McIntyre as breathing the briny air. He'd been stung by jellyfish eight times, surfed the tide during past hurricanes, and pulled in a shark on his rod and reel fishing from the jetties. He knew the Historic Strand District by heart and which restaurants were worthy of his hard-earned dollars. And his wife, Cecelia, had birthed their child at John Sealy Hospital four years ago. *Spencer.* His heart ached at the thought of never seeing his son again.

He closed his eyes in prayer again, but even as he tried to focus on communion with God, fear wrapped around him like a serpent squeezing the life out of him. Wondering what it would feel like to drown, he prayed that God would send an angel to help him make the journey. Maybe even Cecelia.

Alex put her car in park on high ground and dialed 9-1-1. She had seen someone's head barely above the water, leaning against a concrete pillar in the distance, as the water rose around the guy. Her heart hammered in her chest as a recorded message played on her cell phone—*all circuits busy*. She knew better than to wade out in water to her chest with all the debris swirling in fast currents around him. Dialing again, she got the same message. As the rain slowed down, she glimpsed the Christmas wreaths in the distance, lit by the grace of God only, since almost every other area had gone dark from the storm. Each year, decorations seemed to go up earlier. It wasn't even Thanksgiving yet. Clenching her cell phone, she blasted herself for not leaving Galveston sooner. Authorities had given ample warnings to vacate the island, but a hurricane in November? She couldn't recall a storm like this in her lifetime so late in the season.

She'd stayed at the hospital longer than she'd intended, knowing it might be the last time she would see her father. But she had felt that way every day for the past two months after a visit. Sometimes she stayed in her father's room, but she'd forgotten her heart medicine this morning, so she had opted to go home. Missing the meds wouldn't put her health at risk, but her elevated pulse would cause her heart to pound like a base drum in her chest.

Glancing at the man in the water, she walked around to the trunk of her car and searched for a tie strap or bungee cord. She needed something to tie to her car so she could hold onto the other end. If she was going to walk into the floodwaters, she wanted to be able to get back to her car. She wasn't a strong swimmer, and even if she was, the current looked strong enough to sweep her away, a thought that caused her bottom lip to tremble. She wasn't adventuresome by nature, so this potential rescue sent her heart racing even more as she realized the bungee cord she'd found wouldn't be nearly long enough. She tossed it back in the trunk and called 9-1-1 again and jumped when she heard a voice.

"9-1-1. What is your emergency?"

"I'm on Harborside Drive near the cruise terminal, and a

man is trapped in the water. It looks like he's pinned against a concrete pillar."

"What is your name, please?"

Alex scowled. "Alex Hansen. Please hurry."

She paced the length of her car as she detailed her exact location, not taking her eyes off of the man, the water rising to within a few feet of her Honda. If she didn't move her car soon, she was going to be trapped as well. But she couldn't leave a man to drown.

As the winds picked up, more branches floated atop the rushing water that separated her and the stranger, and within a few seconds, the downpour resumed. Water was up to the guy's chin. *Dear Lord, please. What do I do?*

After the 9-1-1 operator came back on the line and said someone was on the way, Alex hit End, tossed the phone on her seat, and locked the car. She opened the door to the gas tank and put her keys inside the compartment before closing it again. Then she took a hesitant step into the water, thankful she'd worn tennis shoes today. The force of the unwelcome seawater gyrated around her ankles, and as she eased forward, it wasn't long before the water was up to her thighs. *Stupid, stupid.* Keeping her eye on the man, while also scanning the area around her, her stomach churned when she thought she saw a snake, but it was only a stick.

With slow steps and sheer will forcing her feet forward, she got within shouting distance of the man, but no matter how much she cried out to him, the wind slammed against her voice, abducting the sound into its wrath. As the guy moved his mouth, she couldn't hear anything he said, but she was within a few yards now, the water to her waist. If she lost her footing, she was going to be swept away. She thought about her father and the irony of the situation if she went before him.

Slow and steady.

The rain eased up again, but the winds fiercely tugged at her, first one way, then the other. She'd lived in Galveston long enough to know how fast the water could rise, so she picked up her pace, trembling but determined.

Her father's strong will and perseverance leapt into the forefront of her mind as she tried to funnel his determination. Richard Hanson believed a person could do anything if their commitment to the task was strong enough. *If you can't fly, then run. If you can't run, then walk. If you can't walk, then crawl. But whatever you do, you have to keep moving forward.* It was something she'd heard her father recite many times, a quote by Martin Luther King, Jr.

"You shouldn't have come," the man said when she finally reached him, his face pale, his eyes wide. "My leg is pinned. You need to go back."

"Too late!" she yelled above the roar of the wind. *Stay with me, Lord.* She stuck her head underneath the water, but it was thick as Texas fog, and she couldn't see anything. When she lifted her head, the sting of mascara in her eyes distracted her for a few moments as she blinked and dabbed at her eyes with her wet ZZ Top T-shirt. She jumped when she felt something brush against her foot, an unidentifiable object that stung as it passed by her. A branch, maybe. It felt like a deep paper cut. "I called 9-1-1, but who knows how long it will take for them to get here, or if they can even get through. We need to get you to my car somehow."

He shook his head. "I can't get my leg free. The higher the water got, the harder I've tried."

Alex glanced around as the skies spit a light trickle of rain, but the wind was like a dozen tornadoes funneling around them. As two large branches drifted by, she silently asked God for help again.

"Do you have any idea what has you pinned? A branch or something?" She ran her fingers underneath her eyes, hoping to clear the blackness she was sure the mascara had left. It seemed an odd time to notice the man's square jaw, intense blue eyes, and a dimple on one side only. She wondered what the rest of him looked like beneath the water. Was he tall? He was crouched in the water, so it was hard to tell. If she didn't clear her mind, he was going to drown.

"I don't know. I thought it was a branch, but I'm not really sure." His voice was gargled, like maybe he'd already swallowed water, and there was an urgency in his tone that caused a jolt of adrenaline to rush through Alex's veins and slam against her chest.

"I'm guessing you are in a lot of pain?" She flinched when he did.

He latched onto her arm. "Listen . . ." He spoke loudly, against the roar of the wind. "You must get back to your car and get out of here. Go now, while you can. I'm sure someone will show up soon, and they'll have equipment to get me out."

Alex eyed the water that was now up to his bottom lip as she stood towering above him. Swallowing hard, she took a deep breath. If she left him, she'd see his face in her dreams —nightmares—for the rest of her life. "I'm not leaving you here. What's your name?" He was breathing faster as he struggled to hold his head higher.

"Parker. Listen . . ." he said again, breathing hard. "I have a son, Spencer. Please find him, and you tell him that Daddy went to be with Mommy, and tell him . . . tell him I love him with everything I am, and—"

"Stop! You're not going to die. I'll get you out of here." Alex heard the shakiness in her voice. In the corner of her eyes she saw the street lights go out, along with the festive strings of Christmas lights connecting them. The wreaths dangling from the middle of the display shone brightly, which seemed odd to Alex.

Parker shook his head. "No. I'm stuck." He was still clutching her arm. "Please promise me that you'll find my son. His aunt got him safely off the island earlier today, but when it's safe, please find him, tell him . . ." His voice trailed off as he let go of her arm. A wave slammed into his face, filling his mouth with water, and the more he sputtered, the more he choked. He was breathing way too hard. Alex hadn't had more than basic first-aid classes, but she could tell he was panicking.

"How old is Spencer?" She bent at the waist and put her face closer to his until he finally locked eyes with her, a rhythmic set of mini rapids swooshing between and around them.

"Four," he said barely loud enough for Alex to hear as he

lifted his chin higher. "Dear, God . . ." he whispered, closing his eyes. His hand found Alex's and he squeezed. "Will you pray with me?"

Alex had been praying since she took her first step into the rushing river of saltwater that was rising. "Yes," she said as she cupped his cheek with her other hand. "Dear Lord, please give us the courage and strength to free Parker from whatever is holding him in the water. Please, God . . ."

"No . . . I need to . . ." More water found its way into Parker's mouth, followed by more choking. Alex waited while he caught his breath again. "I—I ask you God to forgive my trespasses, my sins . . ."

Alex scanned the area as best she could. Not a soul in sight. Floodwater had risen halfway up the tires of her Honda. She was wise enough to know that if Parker went completely underwater, he would likely grab onto her in a panic, possibly taking her underwater also. She'd no sooner had the thought when the rains began to subside. There was still a fierce wind, but maybe they were buying some time. *Thank you, God.* She also thought she heard a siren in the distance.

"Tell me your name," Parker said as his teeth chattered. It wasn't cold, so she wasn't sure what was happening. These first couple of weeks in November had been unseasonably warm.

"Alex. Short for Alexandria."

The hint of a smile played across his lips. "You're a brave woman, Alexandria."

"No one calls me that, except for my father." She thought

again about the man she loved most in the world. "And I'm not really brave, but I'm not leaving you."

Parker held her gaze. "Yes, you will. And you *should*. You should go now."

Alex shook her head. "No. We aren't giving up. Help is on the way."

Parker smiled a little again. "If you can't fly, then run. If you can't run, then walk. If you can't walk, then crawl. But whatever you do, you have to keep moving forward."

Alex froze, stopped breathing for a few seconds. "Martin Luther King, Jr."

"Yes." He let out a long, controlled sigh. "A good man."

Alex's eyes filled with tears. There was no doubt in her mind that her father had died. She didn't know how she knew, but she did. *He was another good man.*

"What's wrong?" Parker waved an arm atop the rapids around them. "Besides the obvious?"

"My father just died." She wasn't sure why she blurted it out to a stranger, but she was confident in her statement, and within seconds, she was crying.

Parker's fingers brushed against hers beneath the water and found her palm, intertwining his fingers with hers. "I'm so sorry. When? Recently?"

Just now. She couldn't tell him that. "Yes."

He squeezed her hand. "Alexandria, I am very sorry for your loss."

"Thank you."

They were quiet for a few moments, and there was actually a trickle of sunlight peeking through the clouds.

"The eye of the storm," Parker said, a tinge of hope in his voice. "It's not even that big of a hurricane."

Alex swiped at her eyes, drawing back black fingertips. "Mascara. I probably look like a raccoon."

Parker was still holding her hand. "You are the most beautiful raccoon I've ever seen."

"Oh, I'm sure I am," she said, trying to smile, needing to lighten the fear and strengthen her resolve.

Alex had noticed how handsome he was earlier. She'd learned a long time ago to never get too attracted to someone who was sitting down, or in Parker's case—hunched over in dangerous floodwaters. Alex was five-foot-ten. She recalled meeting Jimmy Strasburg on a blind date in college. He had arrived at the agreed upon meeting place before she did, and he was already seated. They talked for two hours, got along wonderfully. Then Jimmy stood up. He couldn't have been an inch over five-foot-two, and with her heels on, Alex had towered over him like an island palm tree when they'd left the restaurant. It was silly. Height certainly shouldn't define a person, but she supposed everyone had dating requirements. Five-ten or taller was one of hers.

A gust of wind sent a rushing surge of water over Parker's face, and when his face was visible again, his wide eyes revealed his panic as he coughed water, straining to raise his chin higher. It started to rain again, and Alex's stomach lurched. But she needed him still and calm.

"Do you have plans for the holidays? Thanksgiving isn't far away." She hoped her voice sounded steadier than it felt.

"I know you're trying to make small talk so I won't panic." He took in a gulp of air before water splashed across his face again.

Alex winced as he squeezed her hand underwater. "Is it working?"

His expression stilled. "What are the chances that I would be here, in this predicament, with you, and that you'll be the last person I'll see on this earth?"

"Do. Not. Give. Up." She turned in every direction, but didn't see anyone, and the siren she'd thought she heard earlier was either gone or she'd imagined it. "Help is coming."

"My son lost his mother, and it seems unfair that he's going to lose me, too, without getting to know either one of us very well."

Parker seemed to be settling in on the fact that he was going to die. Only once had Alex ever faced death head on. She'd had a severe reaction to an antibiotic that had left her covered from head to toe with a nasty rash that would eventually take months to recover from. But it was the threat of Stevens-Johnson syndrome that had terrified her at the time. She could still recall the look on the doctor's face when she'd asked, "Can this kill me?" The female dermatologist had nodded. Up until that point, she'd always thought her faith was solid, but when faced with her own demise, she'd been terrified. The way Parker was now.

The rain pounded them now with a relentless vengeance, large pellets battering and bouncing off their heads like dull needles against a pincushion. Waves were pushing forward with a force that could only come with a rising tide, and as Alex saw a large sheet of plywood float by in the water, she wondered how much more dangerous and heavy debris was floating by beneath the surface of the tenebrous waters.

"You're not going to die," she said with as much conviction as she could, but as the water rose higher and higher, Parker could barely fend off the swells pushing into his mouth. *Please, God.*

Parker stared into Alex's eyes, longing to see his soul in the reflection, wondering if it would be an easy trip to the other side, and praying he would be going in the right direction. He'd heard stories about people seeing loved ones right before they passed to the next life, whispering their names as they drifted over. He searched this woman's eyes again, looking for Cecelia, but all he saw was the terror in Alex's eyes. He owed this stranger more than he'd ever be able to give her.

"The moment my nose and mouth are underwater, turn and look away. Go quickly . . ." He paused, holding his mouth closed as a wave of water lapped all the way to his forehead before receding. "Go quickly to your car. Don't let my drowning be the very last thing you see." He paused again. "You really should go now."

She shook her head. "No. Help will come."

Bless her for staying, but . . . "Do you have children?" He spoke louder than before so she could hear him above the fierce winds encircling them.

"Nope. Not married, no children. I haven't found the right man yet."

"I find that hard to believe."

She smiled a little. "True story." Her bottom lip trembled as she squeezed his hand.

"What will you do for the holidays?" It was small talk, but Parker's heart was beating way too fast, and if he didn't drown soon, he feared he would have a heart attack. Maybe that would be the lesser of the two evils he faced. A few hours ago, Christmas lights had flickered on the Strand, even though merchants were busy boarding up their windows. Now everything had gone dark. Even the Christmas wreaths that had stayed lit longer than anything else.

"I don't know."

He didn't say anything, took a deep breath, and waited as the water rose above his mouth. He tried to wiggle free of Alex's hold on his hand, but she just clung tighter. He didn't know it was possible to breathe so fast through his nose, and he waited for Cecelia to make herself known. But once again, the water receded to his chin as the wind stilled, which would only be temporary, until the next surge. Parker figured he wouldn't outlast more than a couple more waves.

"It's just been me and my dad for a long time," Alex said. "My mom died when I was young. We spent nearly every holiday at the beach, and always on Christmas day." She was almost screaming now since the winds had picked up, and probably because she was scared. "My house is on Crystal Beach, a little east of Galveston on the Bolivar Peninsula. My dad helped me get it after Hurricane Ike hit in 2008 and we got a really great deal. Everything was kind of a mess for a while, but we both knew it was the only way I'd ever be able to afford a house right on the beach." She shrugged, shaking. "Anyway, we always set up a small table by the sea and ate fish tacos. It might sound silly to some people, but it was our thing. We even wore goofy Christmas hats." Black streaks of mascara trailed down her cheeks. She recalled her father always calling their holiday Christmas by the Sea. "My dad always wanted to be a boat captain, but he worked as a carpenter instead, giving up his own dreams so I would have a normal and happy life." She paused, recalling her idyllic childhood, wondering how she was going to live without her father. Hopefully, her parents were dancing in heaven and would be sharing fish tacos on Christmas day. "It will be my first time to eat tacos on Christmas day by myself."

"I'm sorry about your father." Parker wasn't sure he'd ever felt a connection to another human being the way he did to this woman now. Except maybe his son. And Cecelia. Maybe it was because he was going to die holding her hand. He knew she wouldn't leave until he'd gone still in the water. Even though she should.

Dirty water rushed by them carrying everything from dead fish to floating bags of trash. Two large branches swam atop the rapids, followed by a Burger King bag, an empty toilet paper roll, and a couple of empty cups with straws protruding from the lids. The pain in his leg had subsided to a dull ache, but his chest had tightened to the point he almost couldn't breathe. Then it happened.

A big rush of water.

He clamped his mouth closed, but when it receded, it only receded to just below his nostrils. The next surge would be it. Alex was crying as she held his hand, but then she jerked away from him, turned, and started struggling against the current to get to her car. He couldn't say a word because she was doing exactly what he'd told her to do. But if he'd been able to talk, he would have begged her to stay. He closed his eyes and prayed.

Seconds later, her hand was on his arm, and she was holding a paper cup that had floated by. One ear remained barely above the water, and Parker heard sirens. Or was he imagining it? Glancing to his left, he thought he'd seen movement. *Cecelia?* He thought he heard Christmas music.

"I know you can hear me, but can't speak, so listen." Alex spoke firmly, as if this was the most important thing she was ever going to say in her life. "Your nose is going to go underwater soon, but you can breath through this straw as long as the other end stays above the water. I hear sirens. Help is close. So, don't panic." She lowered the straw into the water, her finger plugging the end that Parker eased into his mouth, wrapping his lips around it and her finger before she slowly took her hand away. He filled his lungs with a long breath of air, trying hard not to panic.

Parker heard the sirens. *They're coming.* He did his best to force himself calm, and just as she'd said, the water rose above his nose. Clamping his nostrils closed with one hand, he clung to her other hand as he breathed through the straw.

Too big of a wave would cause him to intake water, panic, and she'd never get the straw back in his mouth. It seemed odd that he would have such a rational thought, but as Spencer's face flashed in his mind's eye, he prayed for God to keep his breathing steady.

As the tide that engulfed them continued to rise, only a couple of inches of the straw cleared the water. His new friend was going to lose this heroic battle.

When the straw slipped from his mouth, he held his breath, but it was only seconds before he gagged and water began to fill his lungs. The space around him went black, and finally . . . there was Cecelia. Smiling. Floating nearby. Her arms open. But Spencer's face bounced around his mind, the reminder of all that he was leaving behind. Parker felt like he was crying, but it was hard to tell. His body was going limp. Total darkness. *Where is the light? Why is there no light? Where did Cecelia go? Where is Alex?* She'd seen him die, or so she thought, so she'd fled. *Good.* Maybe she'd left before all the thrashing started. *Did I thrash?* He wasn't sure.

Then a surge of horrific pain engulfed his lower leg, and he was sure his foot was being sawed off with a dull, serrated knife. But he was too tired to struggle. *Too dead*, he assumed.

Alex cringed as she ducked below the dirty water and wrapped both arms around Parker's legs, pulling with all her might as blood circled and swooshed around them like the scene of a shark attack. She eventually tugged hard enough to get him loose and was able to get his head above water, but his body was limp, heavy like dead weight. *Is he dead?*

As she struggled to hold onto him from behind and keep his head above water, she repeatedly lost her footing, twice almost losing them both to the wrath of the current. The sirens were getting closer, but she wasn't sure she could hold him for much longer. Ferocious winds churned the fast-moving water into a sea of rapids carrying even more debris. Tears, mixed with mascara and saltwater, burned her eyes as long strands of hair whipped across her face in every direction. *Please God, help me to hold onto him.* When her legs began to tremble, she didn't think she had enough energy left to fight the current, and there was a burning sensation below her knee, along with eddies of blood. *His or hers*, she wondered?

In the distance, her Honda Civic was giving up the fight. Alex's heart pounded against the wall of her chest as the water lifted the car from the elevated spot where she'd parked, carrying it away—along with whatever hope she had left. But then she saw headlights, and with a burst of super-power, she tightened her grip on Parker and fought shaky legs as tears drizzled down her cheeks. Two men emerged from a pickup truck, and not far behind there was an ambulance.

"Stay where you are!" One of the men secured a belt of some type around his waist, while the other one hooked the other end to the bumper of the truck. The vehicle was much further away than where Alex had left her car; that entire area was submerged now.

The man covered the distance between the truck and Alex

in less than a minute, but with slow and steady steps as the water rushed around him.

"It's him. He's the one really hurt." Alex heard the shakiness in her voice and felt the rattle in her throat, but when the rescuer took over, she fought not to melt into the current.

A few minutes later, they were on high ground, and two paramedics took over, administering CPR to Parker while the original two guys, presumably volunteers, cleaned up the cut on Alex's leg. But she never took her eyes off of Parker, praying that he'd wake up.

Finally, he sputtered water, but when he became fully conscious, his blood pressure was so high, the paramedics called the hospital, asking permission to give Parker something to ease the pain. Within a few minutes, he was comfortably sleeping in the back of the ambulance. The rain had slowed, as if God had a protective umbrella over them.

"Can I ride in the ambulance with him?" Alex touched his foot, the one that wasn't injured and the only part of his body she could reach from where she was standing.

"We don't have room. There's another emergency up the road." One of the breathless paramedics climbed inside the ambulance and sat next to Parker. "We need the room, but if you're his wife . . . can you follow us?"

Alex shook her head. "I'm not his wife, but my car washed away while all of this was going on, and—"

"We can give you a ride to wherever you need to go." It was

the man who had braved the current to rescue Alex and Parker.

She glanced back and forth between the paramedic still standing at the back of the ambulance and the man who had saved hers and Parker's lives. "Can we follow the ambulance to the hospital?"

"Sure."

Alex took another long look at Parker before the doors closed. "Is he going to be okay?"

The paramedic nodded. "Yeah, I believe so. His foot is in pretty bad shape, but all of his vitals are stable. His blood pressure was probably high from the pain, but I think he will be all right."

Alex took a long cleansing breath, then walked with the two volunteers to their truck. Water was already inching up the tires. They'd barely cleared the hazardous area when one of them took a phone call, and it was easy enough for Alex to tell from one side of the conversation that they weren't going to the hospital.

The passenger in the front seat looked over his shoulder at Alex. "I'm sorry Ma'am, we've got another emergency, so we can't follow the ambulance to Houston right now."

Alex nodded. "I understand. I have a friend who lives nearby if you want to drop me there, or I'll ride with you to wherever you need to go." She shivered at the thought of being at any other accident scene. But the passenger made a quick phone call, then turned back to Alex. "Where does your friend live?"

After she'd explained, the man nodded and turned to the

driver. "We should be able to avoid heavy flooding to get her to friend's place. Jim and Marty are almost to the other emergency. Let's drop her at her friend's house."

"Thank you," she said barely above a whisper, but then she cleared her throat. "Do you know what that man's last name was, the one they took away in the ambulance?"

One man shook his head while the other said, "No. I didn't even hear his first name."

Alex wished she'd asked Parker his last name, but she assumed they were taking him to a Houston hospital further inland. She'd find him later. Right now, she had another call to make.

"I hate to even ask this but . . . my father is in John Sealy Hospital, and I urgently need to call him. Would it be possible to borrow a cell phone?" Alex's purse and belongings had been submerged in her car. Sniffling, she couldn't stop trembling, despite the blanket she'd been given after being pulled from the rushing water.

"Sure." The passenger reached over the seat and handed her his phone. They were both young guys, maybe late twenties, around Alex's age. "Call as many people as you need to. You've been through quite an ordeal. But click over if another call comes in." He smiled. "You saved that guy's life."

While my father was dying less than a mile away. She Googled John Sealy Hospital, and a few minutes later, she heard a familiar voice.

"Alex, we've been trying to reach you." Nurse Karen's soft whisper confirmed what Alex already knew to be true.

Moments later, she handed the guy his phone, crying hard now.

"Wow, I'm real sorry for your loss," the driver said, not going more than ten miles an hour, the car swaying in the wind as he did his best through high water. "You've already been through a lot today."

Alex pulled the blanket snug around her, and it wasn't long before her quiet sobs turned to uncontrollable crying. *I'm sorry I wasn't there, Daddy.*

~

Parker swam in and out of consciousness, aware that he was in an ambulance, and later knowing he was in a hospital. His eyes were closed, but the smell of ammonia and beeping machines alerted him as to where he was. Maybe he wasn't going to die after all.

As he stared at the back of his eyelids, it wasn't Cecelia he saw, but the vision of an angel who had rescued him. Her long dark hair swooped in wild strands across her face, black mascara trailing down her cheeks, the fear in her eyes. *Alex.*

He was slipping away again. *Tired. Sleep.*

When he woke up, there were three doctors standing at the foot of the bed, along with his sister—and Spencer. *Thank you, God.* His four-year-old son stood next to Angie, Parker's only sibling.

"Hey, Buddy." Parker held his arm out to his son, who rushed to him, burying his head in the nook of Parker's shoulder. "Daddy's okay," he said in a shaky whisper. He swallowed back the knot in his throat as he clung to his son's love like a life raft. "I'm okay," he repeated softly, as much for himself as for Spencer.

But am I okay? Something felt amiss below his left knee, hollow.

Angie came around the other side, leaned down, and kissed Parker on the cheek. "Welcome back. You've been sleeping for two days."

"Where . . .?" He scanned the room. Three male doctors who didn't look any older than Parker stood quietly. "Where is the woman, the one who helped me?"

"I don't know anything about her," the shortest of the young doctors said, as if Alex was just a random person of no consequence. "But we do need to talk to you, Mr. McIntyre." The guy—Dr. Easton, his badge read—glanced at Angie, who quickly went to the other side of the bed.

"Hey, Spence," she said softly. "Let's take a walk while the doctors talk to Daddy."

His son clung tightly to Parker's arm, but eventually let Angie take him out of the room.

This is bad. He waited, searching each of the three men's faces for a clue. The short doctor cleared his throat. He seemed to be the one in control. The boss.

"You're going to be fine, Parker, but the damage to your foot was extensive, and we were unable to repair the cartilage. I'm afraid we had to perform an amputation a few inches below your knee. But the good news is that you are a strong candidate for a prosthetic device once the area has healed."

Parker's heart thumped against his chest in a way that

caused his vision to blur. The next thing he knew, a nurse was in the room putting a shot of something in his IV, nothing strong enough to keep him from throwing back the covers on his bed. He couldn't remember the last time he'd cried prior to the accident, but now he bawled like a baby. There was a huge white bandage, a stump. *I don't have a foot.*

Darkness again. *Did someone turn out the light? Or am I seeing the back of my eyelids?*

His heart stopped pounding, the heaviness lifted.

Alex spent two days on her friend's couch in Galveston. Gina's apartment building had stayed high and dry, despite the continued rains and flooding. Alex focused on finding Parker. She'd used Gina's phone to check hospitals, but she hadn't been able to find him. *Difficult without a last name.*

When some of the roads cleared, Alex's best friend, Shelley, picked her up and took her back to her apartment in Houston since there wasn't a clear route to Alex's house yet. They stopped at Walmart on the way to pick up a cheap cell phone since Alex's had been lost when her car was washed away. Alex continued her search for Parker with no luck. She'd called every hospital on the outskirts of Galveston, most of them full and overflowing with patients who had been relocated prior to the storm. Her father had been deemed too critical to move, and he'd been taken to the safest wing of the hospital during the storm. *Only to die anyway.*

"Still no word on the guy?" Shelley Armstrong sipped on a

Red Bull next to Alex on the couch, her bare feet on the coffee table while videos of the aftermath of the storm scrolled across the television. Most of the water had receded, but the devastation was massive.

Alex and Shelley had grown up together, but Shelley had made the move to Houston when she landed a job working as a paralegal for a law firm. Alex had been fortunate to find work on the island as a human resources manager for a large hotel chain.

"No. I still haven't been able to find him." Alex was desperate to learn what happened to Parker, and she'd chastised herself repeatedly for not getting his last name. She had watched the news on television since she'd been staying at Shelley's, hoping for a glimpse of her car, a mention about Parker, or anything that might help her to locate him. But nothing. No one was being let back onto the island, and Alex's father was in the morgue at John Sealy Hospital. She'd been crying on and off since she'd arrived at Shelley's apartment.

"When things calm down, I bet you'll be able to find him." Shelley put a hand on Alex's leg and patted her twice, as if everything would be okay. Alex wasn't sure things would ever be alright. She had nightmares. Parker's wild eyes when he went underwater. Her Herculean strength as she tore his leg from whatever held it beneath the water. Keeping him upright in a current that should have swept them both away. The medical personnel intercepting him, pushing Alex out of the way. Her not being able to ride in the ambulance.

She picked up her cell phone. She had eight more hospitals to try, even though she'd already called the closest ones to

Galveston, and now she was trying hospitals way on the other side of Houston. Seven calls later, and still no luck. But she dialed the number for the eighth one on the list. *Please God, I've got to find him.*

Two weeks later, Parker was released from the hospital, even though there would be all kinds of follow-up appointments and rehab. Angie packed his things as he stared at the wheelchair by the bed. Eventually, he would advance to crutches, and then if all went well, he'd be fitted for a prosthetic leg.

"The guy I talked to at your office—Jake—said there isn't a rush to get back to work," Angie said. "He said to take your time."

Parker nodded. He'd talked to Jake during his hospital stay, but for some reason, the phone in his room wasn't working today, and he wasn't getting good cell service either. "Thanks for calling him. Where's Spencer?" Parker sat up in bed and slung his legs over the side. His one-and-a-half legs.

"Maryanne, a nurse where I work has two children close to Spencer's age, and she's off today. Great people. I thought it might be good for Spencer to have some playtime while we get you settled at the condo, then I'll pick him up.

Parker's temporary home would be a condo in Houston. He disliked Houston. Too busy. He couldn't smell the ocean, watch the boats come in, or walk the beach. Although he wouldn't be walking anywhere soon.

He wondered how long it would be before he'd be back in his house. Mostly he wondered why he hadn't been able to find a woman named Alexandria who lived at Crystal Beach. He was angry with himself for not getting her last name. And to his recollection, he hadn't given her his full name either.

As he thought about Spencer, he knew that he would forever be in debt to a woman named Alex who had made sure he lived, at great personal risk to herself. Her face was etched into his brain forever. The fear. The determination. The . . . beauty.

They had prayed together, and he'd been sure her face would be the last one he'd see in this life. But now, he couldn't find her, and doing so was a top priority.

"Did you tell Jake about the two files in my desk drawer?" Parker stared at the white lump of bandages a few inches below his knee. It didn't hurt anymore. It was just a void. *I don't have a foot anymore.* But he'd tried to keep his life organized as best he could from the hospital, and making sure his boss had two client files was a part of that effort.

"Yeah, I did." Angie zipped a small, red suitcase she'd brought him early on. A few clothes, socks, toothbrush, and a Bible. Two hospital chaplains had been by twice each, to talk to Parker about how blessed he was, citing those who had lost their lives in the storm. Parker didn't need convincing. He knew he was blessed. He'd lost his foot, and that was something that didn't come easily. He'd gone through the expected range of emotions, from sadness to anger to acceptance. But he was alive. And he was going to see his son grow into a man, good Lord willing.

"Are you sure you don't want me to stay with you a while at the rental?" Angie sighed as she set the packed suitcase by the door.

"No. I'll be able to drive soon. My condo is on the first floor. And I know you're a phone call away."

"You can't drive *yet*." Angie's voice had a firm, but gentle, tone to it. She reminded him of their mother when she talked like she was now.

Their parents were on an extended vacation, or an early retirement. Parker and Angie weren't sure, but at the moment, Mom and Dad were with a tour group in Spain, not expected to be home until after the holidays. Parker had to talk his mother out of getting on the next plane home. His parents had saved money and made plans to spend this year traveling, and Parker had repeatedly explained to his mom that Angie had things under control, that they should carry on with their vacation. They could continue to Skype, and Parker promised to keep his parents updated on his progress, assuring them that he was okay and would learn to function without the lower part of one leg. *Eventually*.

He'd mostly moved past the angry phase, but those emotions still reared up occasionally. When they did, it was Parker's first instinct to lash out at God. Instead, he forced himself to stow any rage and to thank the Lord for sparing his life. Spencer was an easy reminder that Parker needed to be grateful.

Poor Spencer would probably never get to do anything exciting in his entire life, since Parker was already overprotective. Losing Cecelia had left Parker feeling like he'd never survive if something happened to Spencer. When he thought about how close he'd come to leaving his son without any parents at all, his thoughts drifted to the woman who had saved his life.

Alex. Where was she?

Alex lay two red roses on her father's grave. The headstone still hadn't arrived, but it had only been a couple of weeks since she'd ordered it. She'd come to visit him every day since the funeral, and now with Thanksgiving only a few days away, she still cried every time she visited. She'd still been searching for Parker, but twenty-three hospitals later, she still had no information. Maybe she was just never meant to know him. She was there, at the right time, at the right moment. *Fate? God's will that they met, never to see each other again?* With each day, she was accepting that reality, although she'd see his eyes, the look before he completely went underwater, for the rest of her life. But she could recall his square jaw and his handsome features too. She wanted to remember him forever, and she was sure she would.

"I'm off to work, Daddy." Alex kissed her fingertips, then pressed them against the dirt of her father's grave, the mound slowly flattening with each of her visits.

Taking a deep breath, she got in her rental car, an ugly dark green Camry that her insurance company provided. She'd gotten a new drivers license, Social Security card, and replaced other items she'd lost during the flood. The loss of life had hit a hundred, and there were still dozens in Galveston hospitals and other facilities in Houston. Most of those killed were the ones who hadn't left the island, the old timers who had survived many a hurricane, some as far back as Hurricanes Alicia and Carmen. Both before Alex's time.

She'd just started driving toward the cemetery exit when she heard music coming from her purse. She put her foot on the brake and dug around inside her bag until she found the phone and answered.

"You're still coming for Thanksgiving, right?" Shelley was hosting her entire family in her small apartment for the holiday. Alex wasn't sure how she'd fit even one more person. Shelley said she was expecting eighteen.

"Yeah, I'll be there. Thanks, Shelley."

Alex would have preferred to sit on the beach and eat tacos with her father, watch the boats, the waves, and inhale the briny smells of an ocean they both loved, but that wasn't going to happen this year. Shelley had been insistent that Alex spend the holiday with her and her family, and maybe it was best Alex not be alone on this first holiday without her beloved father.

Hopefully, her father had found her mother and they were both gazing upon a great ocean in heaven, eating all the fish tacos that they could consume.

And hopefully Alex would start to feel normal again some day.

It was the first week of December when Parker walked across his living room, receiving applause from his son and Angie. The prosthetic half-leg was temporary, but it gave him mobility he hadn't had until now, and he was thankful. Eventually, he'd have a custom fit prosthesis. He was also grateful that Angie had put up a Christmas tree in his condo, decorated it, and filled it with gifts underneath. Angie didn't have a lot of money. Nurses were extremely underpaid. He realized that even more after his accident. But Angie packed every single thing individually, even if it was something small from the Dollar Store. She'd wrap it in a big box, and every year, the amount of presents under the tree grew, giving them an exaggerated vision of the amount of money she spent on gifts. But the focus had always been on family and blessings, something beautiful that their parents had passed down during their modest childhoods. Parker was glad his folks had been able to save some money over the years, enough to travel the way they'd always planned.

"Are we going to go see Santa today?" Spencer's toothy smile stretched across his precious face, his bright blue eyes anxious to experience the season. This year more than ever, Parker was excited to watch his son open presents.

"Um, I need to ask you something." Angie took a deep breath and blew it out slowly.

What now? She'd already helped him battle it out with the health insurance company about services that providers had deemed unnecessary. She'd also been the one to inform him that his deductible was five thousand dollars. Parker couldn't recall being sick prior to this, so he hadn't ever looked closely at his policy, which was proving to be a nightmare. But when his sister smiled, he thought he caught a twinkle in her eyes. "What?" he finally asked.

"I know we said we were going to have a quiet Christmas

together, just you, me, and Spencer at my apartment, since Mom and Dad are traveling, but . . ." Yep, there was a twinkle in his sister's eyes. "Do you mind if someone else joins us?" She folded her hands in front of her, another gesture that reminded Parker of their mother. "His name is Joe."

Parker grinned. "*Joe?*"

Angie nodded, smiling. His sister had been married before, for a total of six months. Parker recalled wanting to beat the guy to a pulp for cheating on Angie, taking the little bit of money she'd saved, and filing for divorce. But Angie had been the stronger one when they were growing up, and she still was, even during her own divorce.

"Of course, *Joe* can come." Parker wanted his sister happy, and if Joe would brighten her holidays, Parker was all for it.

Angie sat down on the couch next to him. "Joe's great, Parker." Grinning like a schoolgirl, she added, "Handsome . . . and he's a doctor."

"Really?" Parker's smile grew. "Not too surprising, I guess, since you're a nurse."

She cleared her throat as she sat taller on the couch twisting to face him. "Actually, he was one of *your* doctors when you were in the hospital. I didn't meet him at the hospital where I work."

"Oh." Parker raised an eyebrow. "Which one?"

Angie smiled. "He was with the group of doctors who first told you that they'd had to amputate your foot."

"The short guy or one of the other ones?"

"He isn't that short." Angie grimaced a little, but it didn't last long. His sister wasn't all that tall anyway, and she was giddy and glowing again within a few seconds.

"Of course you can invite your new doctor boyfriend for Christmas." He leaned back against the couch and propped his fake leg up on the coffee table. Angie had told him repeatedly not to call it a fake leg, so the phrase was something Parker had taken up only in his mind.

She locked eyes with him, smiling. "Thanks, Parker." She gave him a hug, then stood up. "I'm going to go." She went to Spencer, kissed and hugged him, then headed to the door, turning to face him before she left. "I know you'll find someone special too."

Parker smiled. He already had. He just couldn't locate her.

Alex carried two folding chairs from her house to the beach. She'd tried to ignore the holiday all together, but by the end of the day, she was resolved to revisit her family tradition, if only to carry it on for a final time. She set up the chairs, then went back to the house to retrieve the small table that she'd been putting between the reclining seats for years. In Texas, Christmas was either shorts and T-shirts or down jackets. The temperature varied year to year, ranging within thirty degrees. This year, it was somewhere in between. Not cold enough for a jacket, but not warm enough for shorts. Jeans and a short-sleeve shirt, with a light jacket nearby.

She opened the bag of fish tacos, the ones from a small shack up the road. The place wasn't open on Christmas Day, but Alex always picked up the tacos the day before for her and her father. Biting into one of the tacos, she stared out at the sea as the sun began its descent. Two boats were in the far distance, the waves were calm, and all of the beach debris from the storm had been cleared. She'd only had minor damage to her house and was able to get back in it a few days after the storm, but some homes—those not high enough and sturdy enough—were still undergoing repairs. But not today. Not on Christmas.

She closed her eyes, savoring the taste of the scrumptious taco as the light breeze carried the smell of the ocean, wafting up her nostrils like a familiar friend. She'd visited her father's grave earlier in the day, but otherwise chosen to stay home, despite Shelley's attempts to get her out of the house on Christmas. But the day had been filled with Christmas movies on TV, memories of her father, and now —the greatest fish tacos on earth.

"I miss you, Dad." She held up a champagne glass filled with sparkling grape cider. "Merry Christmas."

The beach was quiet, one of the best things about having Christmas tacos on the beach on Christmas Day. She picked up her Christmas hat, glancing at the one in the empty chair next to her. It was silly and wonderful. Alex had bought the hats during a time when her father was having chemo and had lost his hair. They'd had so much fun wearing them, that they'd worn them every year since. Alex figured she'd retire them after this year, stash the hats in her mother's cedar chest. But as a tribute to her father, she sat on the beach eating tacos and wearing her Santa hat. She set the other hat in the chair next to her. But a movement down the beach caught her eye.

"Ugh," she said through a mouthful. It was a guy. He was by

himself. And he was likely going to want to make small talk, or tell her some horrific story about why he was by himself on Christmas. All of which would mess up the little bit of the day she had left. Behind him, there was another couple and a child.

She picked up an emergency book she'd brought, a habit she'd long ago adopted, even when it wasn't Christmas and she just wanted to be alone on the beach. Burying her head in it, she could feel him approaching, but she didn't look up. Until he stopped right in front of her.

"Hello, Merry Christmas," she said with a mouthful of taco, her head still in the book. Hopefully, he'd get the hint and just walk away.

"Merry Christmas."

Alex's eyes slowly lifted, her mouth stuffed with food. Her heart skipped a beat as she locked eyes with a familiar face. She dropped her taco in the sand as she slowly stood up.

"It's you," she said as she struggled to swallow what was in her mouth, her knees weak, her heart thudding in her chest. "It's you," she repeated as she walked closer to him and smiled. "I looked for you." The words barely whispered across her lips as her eyes filled with tears. "I looked for you," she said again softly.

"I was here Thanksgiving, but I couldn't walk very well at the time, and I couldn't find you. You said you and your father had shared holidays on the beach, so I took a chance." He shrugged a little, grinning. "And I took another chance today, which certainly paid off. I've been looking for you too."

Alex stood up, knowing she must look a wreck and probably had taco sauce on her chin. She gave it a quick swipe, but she couldn't stop smiling. "You're tall."

Parker chuckled. "Yeah, since I was about fourteen."

"Are you . . . did you . . . recover okay?" She looked Parker up and down. He was in jeans and a white T-shirt, wearing tennis shoes.

"Sort of." He lifted his left pant leg, revealing a leg that wasn't the one he was born with.

"Oh no." Alex covered her face with her hands as she shook her head. "I'm so sorry. I'm so very sorry. I—I . . ."

Strong hands landed on top of hers. He eased them away from her face as they stood facing each other. "How could you be sorry? You saved my life."

"But your foot." She looked down again, his pant leg now covering the prosthetic. "It's gone."

"Yep. Gone." He grinned. "It was just a foot."

She appreciated that he was trying to make light of it, but it had to have been devastating. Rarely speechless, Alex stared into his crystal blue eyes.

He brushed back strands of her hair that had swept across her face, then straightened her Santa hat, smiling. "I almost didn't recognize you without raccoon eyes." Inching closer, he said, "Nothing would have ever been right in my universe if I hadn't been able to find you, to thank you for saving my life."

A tear trickled down Alex's cheek, and she didn't bother to swipe it away. She'd never given up seeing Parker again, but a surreal feeling swept over her as he stepped even closer. She leaned up, breathing in his musky scent and the smell of something minty on his breath. But instead of kissing her, he put his arms around her and pulled her head to his broad chest, hugging her tightly. "It's you," he said in a whisper.

"It's you," she repeated easing away from him to look him in the eyes again, to make sure she wasn't dreaming. Then she reached down and picked up her father's Santa hat and handed it to him.

"Are you sure? I know it was your dad's." He paused. "A special time for the two of you."

She nodded, smiling, feeling the same bond she'd felt with him in the water. He leaned down, and she put the hat on him. "You look great," she said, sniffling.

"So do you," he said as he adjusted the hat on his head. "Now." He smiled. "I'd like to know if you'd like to go out with me? On a date."

Alex couldn't wipe the grin from her face as the wind swirled around them in a cool and comforting way, as if repaying them for the hurricane. Bursts of sunlight met with the horizon in a postcard vision of possibilities for the future. "I would like that."

He cupped her chin. "I should probably warn you. I'm not going to wait until a formal goodbye after a date to kiss you. It's going to happen right now."

Alex swallowed hard. "I'm not strong enough to fight you off," she said, grinning.

"Oh, I'm fairly sure you could run away without me being able to catch you." He glanced down at his leg, grinning.

Alex didn't wait for him to make the move. She leaned up and kissed him with everything she had, totally prepared for the entire past event to flash before her in nightmarish visions. But instead, God gifted her with something else. A flash of a future that she could have with this man. They kissed again, then she eased away, staring into his eyes again before they turned to face the ocean, his arm protectively around her. Movement to their right caused them to shift their stance. A small boy was skipping toward them ahead of two adults, his blond hair blowing in the wind as he playfully slowed his stride to kick the sand, leaning down to pick up an occasional shell.

"Awe, he's cute." Alex let her eyes soak in the innocence of youth, carefree and happy. Then she turned back to Parker, silently thanking God for this magical moment.

"He's mine," Parker said, grinning.

Alex brought a hand to her chest and gasped. "Spencer?"

"Yep. The two stragglers behind him are my sister and her new boyfriend."

"Wow." Alex eyed the small boy, his eyes bright as he swung his arms in the air. "He is so adorable."

Spencer stopped in front of them, breathing hard, with something in his hand. "Is this the lady, Daddy?"

Parker bent at the waist. "Yep. This is the pretty lady who saved me."

Alex still had a hand on her chest, but she was certain not a soul on earth could wipe the smile from her face. "Hello, Spencer. I am so happy to meet you." She extended her hand after a few seconds, not sure what protocol was for a boy his age. But Spencer latched on and gave her hand a firm shake, then offered her what was in his other closed hand, dangling it at arm's length.

"What's this?" She opened her palm, still smiling, as she glanced at Parker, then back at Spencer.

He dropped a shell into her hand. "It's for you."

"Thank you very much." She examined the small conch shell. "It's lovely."

Spencer's twinkling blue eyes, the same color as his father's, met Alex's. He blinked a few times as a questioning expression filled his sweet face.

"Are you having Christmas by the sea?"

Warmth filled Alex's soul. She hadn't heard anyone ever use that phrase, besides her father. "Yes, I guess you could say I am."

Spencer scratched his nose as he found his father's gaze. "Maybe we can have Christmas by the sea with Alex sometime."

Parker and Alex exchanged glances, both smiling. Parker said, "I think I'd like that Spencer."

Alex nodded, and Spencer skipped away toward Parker's sister and boyfriend. Parker put his arm around Alex and pulled her close, both of them looking out across the ocean, soaking in the majestic feel of the sea.

And somehow, without a doubt, Alex knew that there would be many more Christmases by the sea. With Parker. And Spencer.

TURN THE PAGE TO READ A SAMPLE
OF MESSAGE IN A BOTTLE

Message
in a
Bottle

a
Surf's Up
novella

BETH
WISEMAN

BESTSELLING AUTHOR

Kyle stretched tape across another box, then lifted it from the floor and piled it on top of the others that he had ready to go.

"I can't believe all this stuff was stashed in this small room." Lexie lowered a stack of file folders into a box. "I don't think I had nearly this much in my dorm room." She grinned as she slung long brown hair over her shoulders. "And I'm a girl. We keep everything."

Kyle eyed the organized mess in the place he'd called home over the past four years. "Some of it probably needs to be trashed, but I'll take a closer look at everything once I get settled in my apartment." He handed Lexie the tape. "Just think, you'll be right downstairs from me. No curfews or rules. We can eat pizza at three in the morning, and we won't have to deal with crazy roommates."

Lexie closed the distance between them and pressed her soft lips gently against his. Kyle eased his arms around her and basked in the scent of her flowery perfume. The feel of her mouth on his was a welcome distraction. They'd briefly considered moving in together, but Kyle's Catholic upbringing kept him from choosing that option. They'd done the next best thing: rented apartments close to each other.

"Maybe we should take a break from packing," Kyle whispered in her ear, trailing kisses down her neck.

She wiggled out of his arms. "Behave. We've got to get this done. You've got to be out of here by the end of the day." She walked to the built-in drawers in Kyle's room and tugged the bottom one until it inched open. "Good grief. What is all this?"

Kyle shuffled across the floor in his socks until he was beside her and staring at the massive amount of pictures, ticket stubs, receipts, and other memorabilia crammed in the top drawer. Sighing, he thumbed his way through the first layer. "Keepsakes."

Lexie smiled as she picked up a picture. "Awe, look at you and Aiden. So handsome."

"My mom sent me that the first week I was here, along with a bunch of other pictures." Kyle recalled how homesick he was at that time. "I was probably seventeen in that picture. Aiden was sixteen."

"Baseball players, I see." Lexie brought the photo closer to her face. "You and your brother look a lot alike in this picture, but not so much in person." She reached for a ticket stub that was folded in half and straightened it. Kyle rolled his eyes as she burst out laughing. "Lady Gaga?"

Kyle shrugged as his mind flooded with memories. "Yeah,

well. I wasn't the one who wanted to go see her, but she actually put on a great show."

"Was this your date?" Lexie held up a photo that was right underneath the ticket. Kyle had his arm around the first girl he'd ever loved. Morgan Calhoun. And thoughts of her still caused his heart to race, even though he was sure no one could be in love as much as he and Lexie. There was no doubt in his mind that he'd marry Lexie one day.

"Yeah. That's Morgan." He swallowed hard. "We grew up on the same street, our families went to the same church, and our moms were best friends." He forced a smile. "My first—and only love—before you."

"Kyle Brossmann, do you expect me to believe that there have only been two loves in your life?"

The question made Kyle wonder how many loves had been in Lexie's life, but it really didn't matter. He'd be the one blessed to live with her for the rest of his days. He hoped.

Kyle nodded. "Yep. There was Morgan. And now you." He eased the photo from her hand and studied Morgan's face, the way her blonde hair curled under slightly below her chin, then tapered past her shoulders. She had magnificent brown eyes and a smile that made people like her before she ever uttered a word. And a body that made guys go nuts. Kyle had questioned her interest in him from day one, knowing someone as attractive as Morgan could have dated anyone she wanted.

"She's really pretty. I'm surprised you haven't mentioned her before." Lexie put her head on his shoulder. "How long did you two date?"

Kyle tucked his dark hair behind his ears, knowing he'd have to shed his long locks before he started his new job. "We dated about a year, but we sort of grew into it. Since we'd known each other most of our lives, we were friends way before anything else." He set the picture back in the drawer, forcing thoughts of Morgan away. Five years later, it was still painful to think about her. But Lexie had already found another selfie of Morgan and Kyle at the beach, the murky Gulf of Mexico in the background. Kyle remembered the cloudy day in Galveston. They'd eaten at Shrimp 'N Stuff and walked on the beach. Kyle looked like his face was twice as big as it really was in the picture. But Morgan looked perfect in her pink bikini top and freshly applied lip gloss.

Lexie couldn't seem to pull her eyes away from the photo. That's the affect Morgan had on most people.

"So what happened with you two?"

It was a conversation Kyle didn't want to have, but if he was going to marry Lexie some day, he supposed there shouldn't be any secrets. "It's a crazy story."

Lexie nudged him gently with her elbow, grinning. "I love crazy stories."

Kyle took a deep breath as all the memories he'd fought to suppress came rushing to the surface. He lowered himself to the edge of the mattress, perching on the corner as he began. "Back in high school, I pulled up to Morgan's house in my truck and honked the horn. She rode with me to school every day, even though she had her own car. I waited, honked again, waited some more, then finally went to the front door and knocked. No answer." His heart hammered against his chest, but he figured he might as well get this over with, then he'd pack up his memories for good. Seal them tight with extra tape, keepsakes his grandchildren would find some day and ask, "Who is this woman grandpa is with?" From heaven, he'd whisper, "My first love."

"Then what?" Lexie eased her way to the bed and sat down.

"I looked in the window, and through the sheer drapes, I could see that the living room was empty. I mean, totally empty. No furniture. Nothing." Kyle felt the sweat beads pooling on his forehead, much like five years ago. "I opened the front door, which was unlocked, and I went through the whole house yelling Morgan's name." He turned to face Lexie, pushed the drawer shut with the heel of one foot, then leaned against the dresser. "There was not one piece of furniture in that entire house."

"I'm confused." Lexie tipped her head to one side, frowning. "Did Morgan and her family just pack up in the middle of the night and disappear?"

Kyle tried to calm the churning in his stomach. "That's exactly what happened."

"Where'd they go?"

"No one knows. It was totally bizarre. My mom was devastated. Maybe even more than me. Morgan's mom and my mom had been pregnant at the same time with us, and they'd been best friends long before Morgan or I could even walk. Mom even hired a private detective to try to find them, convinced that some sort of kidnapping or evil was at work. But the guy took Mom's money and never came up with one single clue."

"Wow." Lexie leaned back on the palms of her hands and blew out a big burst of air she'd been holding. "That *is* a crazy story. I bet that's really haunted you over the years."

You have no idea how much. "Yeah, it did." He walked to the bed, sat down beside her, and leaned in for a kiss. "But I have you. And wherever Morgan is, I hope she's well. But she's a part of my past. My future is with you."

But even as Kyle said the words, his thoughts and memories swam in his head like hungry sharks, wondering about Morgan. Where is she now? Is she happy? Did she go to college like they'd planned to do together?

Where are you, Morgan?

TURN THE PAGE TO READ A SAMPLE
OF THE SHELL COLLECTOR'S
DAUGHTER

The *Shell Collector's Daughter*

a *Surf's Up* novella

BETH WISEMAN

BESTSELLING AUTHOR

Epilogue

Carianna sat across the table from God, the way she'd done every Thursday for as long as she could remember. In the backyard of her father's shop, there was an oak tree with limbs that were hundreds of years old—three hundred and twelve God had told her. Protective branches formed a dome over Carianna's head, even though no protection was needed on Thursdays.

Her father's shop was far enough away from the beach that Carianna couldn't hear the breaking of the waves, but it was close enough to inhale the briny smells of the ocean. A perfect breeze swirled amid the branches of the old tree as Carianna took a sip of her raspberry tea. She loved living on Mustang Island, and she loved these visits with God.

"I'm sending someone into your life, Carianna," God said as He lifted His blue cup to His lips. "A man of My choosing, a person to be with you for the rest of your days on Earth."

Carianna frowned as her stomach clenched. "I have my father for that." She stared at God, and without knowing why or how, Carianna knew He was perfect. *Perfect love.* A smile replaced her sour expression. "And I have You."

Her friend set His cup on the worn wooden table, and He folded one hand on top of the other. God's hands were wrinkled, like her father's, and God's gray hair swept sideways in wiry wisps to one side of His tanned face. A face filled with connecting lines, spidery and deep. She believed God to be older than her father, but it was hard to know for sure.

"Yes, Carianna, you have your father here on earth, and you have Me as your heavenly Father. But I'm talking about a different kind of man. This man will love you in a way that will be new and unfamiliar to you."

Carianna tipped her head to one side, pushing back long strands of brown hair that blew in front of her face. "Do I know this man?"

God shook his head. "No. Not yet. But you will feel like you know him the moment you meet him. He is a few years older than you, but as you learn of him, just know that I am always with you, so there is no need to be afraid."

Carianna's heart pounded against her chest. She was twenty-six years old, and even though God said there was no need for fear, her breath caught in her throat. "You mean like a boyfriend?" she finally asked.

God smiled. "Yes, Carianna, that's what I mean."

She shook her head as she pressed a hand to her chest. "I don't think I like this idea."

The Lord reached over and touched Carianna's free hand, and the feel of His touch reassured her that all would be well. God's perfect love was never wrong. Carianna was sure of that.

And yet, fear wrapped around her like a serpent, squeezing the life out of her.

ABOUT THE AUTHOR

Beth Wiseman is the best-selling author of the Daughters of the Promise series and the Land of Canaan series. Having sold over two million books, her novels have held spots on the ECPA (Evangelical Christian Publishers Association) Bestseller List and the CBA (Christian Book Association) Bestseller List. She was the recipient of the prestigious Carol Award in 2011 and 2013.

She is a three-time winner of the Inspirational Readers Choice Award, and an INSPY Award winner. In 2013 she took home the coveted Holt Medallion. Her first book in the Land of Canaan series—*Seek Me With All Your Heart*—was selected as the 2011 Women of Faith Book of the Year. Beth and her husband are empty nesters enjoying country life in South Central Texas.

ACKNOWLEDGMENTS

It takes a group of dedicated people to grasp an idea, then mold it into an entertaining story. I'm blessed to have various teams for my projects.

My idea for A *Tide Worth Turning* was followed up with great editing, so much thanks goes to Natalie Hanemann.

To our team leader on this project—Janet Murphy—you continue to rock, and you are, indeed, irreplaceable. Thank you for everything. xo

Thank you to my BFF Renee' Bissmeyer and to my mother, Pat Isley, for speedily proofing the manuscript so we could meet the publishing deadline. Love you both always and forever.

To *Wiseman's Warriors*, you are the best street team a gal could have. Thank you for your dedication to helping me spread the word about Beth Wiseman books.

And it's an honor to dedicate this novella to Jamie Foley, our newest team member. Jamie, you are a bright light in our world, a talented writer, market savvy, and ridiculously smart. It's a true joy to walk alongside you on your writing journey, and I am deeply appreciative that God sent you our way.

And last, but never least, my heartfelt thanks to God for continuing to bless me with stories to tell.

ALSO BY BETH WISEMAN

Surf's Up Novellas

A Tide Worth Turning

Message In A Bottle

The Shell Collector's Daughter

Christmas by the Sea

Visit www.BethWiseman.com for various novellas and collections. While there, you can join Beth's mailing list where she gives sneak peeks about new books, offers giveaways, and shows readers a behind the scenes glimpse into her writing world.

www.ingramcontent.com/pod-product-compliance
Lightning Source LLC
Chambersburg PA
CBHW060257150626
46556CB00022B/2685